William Joseph Madden

# The reaction from agnostic science

William Joseph Madden

**The reaction from agnostic science**

ISBN/EAN: 9783741192647

Manufactured in Europe, USA, Canada, Australia, Japa

Cover: Foto ©Andreas Hilbeck / pixelio.de

Manufactured and distributed by brebook publishing software
(www.brebook.com)

William Joseph Madden

**The reaction from agnostic science**

THE

# REACTION FROM AGNOSTIC SCIENCE

BY

## REV. W. J. MADDEN,

AUTHOR OF

"DISUNION AND REUNION."

---

Second Revised Edition.

---

ST. LOUIS, MO., 1899.
PUBLISHED BY B. HERDER,
17 SOUTH BROADWAY.

# THE

# REACTION FROM AGNOSTIC SCIENCE

BY

## REV. W. J. MADDEN,

AUTHOR OF

"DISUNION AND REUNION."

---

Second Revised Edition.

---

ST. LOUIS, MO., 1899.
PUBLISHED BY B. HERDER,
17 SOUTH BROADWAY.

To

those whose hearts

are troubled

by the burden and the mystery

of life,

and to those who

say they can not believe,

this book

is kindly dedicated.

# PREFACE.

In another work entitled " *Disunion and Reunion* " which I ventured to publish some time ago (Burns & Oates), the question treated could interest only those who still hold by the Christian name, and still cherish a belief in the fundamental doctrines of Christianity. But unfortunately there is in our day, as is well known, a large class, who while living among Christian populations, and conforming outwardly, and often unconsciously, to the standard of Christian morality, because compelled by custom and convenience to do so, at the same time openly renounce all belief in Christian dogma.

" Our kinsmen in the flesh " and of Christian ancestry, they surely ought to be included in the appeals, now so earnestly made, for religious reunion. And I think a strong appeal may be addressed directly to them, at this moment, by pointing out, that the agnostic science which in our day has been entirely responsible for the prevailing unbelief, has proved unsatisfying and

disappointing in its conclusions; that
there is more unrest among men now than
before it began its destructive criticisms,
and that many of its own prominent pro-
fessors are showing signals of distress. _It
will be practical, also, to bid them weigh
the value and use to men in their every-day.
life of the conclusions of faith as against
the conclusions of unbelief and thence consult for their personal safety.

Such is the simple, and let us hope, useful aim of this book.

It is a short book. I have purposely
kept it short. In a busy age it will have
a better chance of being read.

*Modesto, Cal., 1899.*

# CONTENTS.

---

. ( vii )

## CHAPTER I.

### Need of the Reaction.

As I sit writing this morning there lies before me the smiling scene of a fertile California valley with the famous Lick Observatory crowning Mount Hamilton on the ridge of the Sierras beyond. And the thought has come to me that if some wild and loosened flood burst suddenly over that valley, its devastating waters and the wreck they should leave behind would fittingly illustrate, without much exaggeration, the desolating infidelity that over a hundred years ago broke over more than one country which used to pass as believing in the "argument for things that do not appear." Up to that, men deemed it reasonable to live in a simple trusting faith and bore more equably the toil and the burden of existence. Since then, the air is filled with questionings and doubts, minds are troubled

(9)

and restless, and from the view of many, the promise and sustaining hope of future and of better things have faded away.

But just as there have really been floods in that valley in other days and now its soil is all the richer for their coming, so, perhaps, will the souls of men be better for that other and more disastrous flood when its troubled waters shall have receded. And happily there are, in these later years, unmistakable signs that they are subsiding.

But a little while ago the agnostic scientist, always referred to as "that eminent man of science," was for worldly-minded people the supreme pontiff of all knowledge worth knowing. In pity for a generation whose "intelligence was limited and whose mind was warped by old superstitions that were said to be revealed because they could not be proved," he undertook to explain the universe on a rational and scientific basis. A tone of superiority and secure self-confidence marked all his pronouncements. His style was magisterial. The crowd like that. It is imposing. Here are men, they say, who make you feel they are sure of what they teach; let us listen to them; and they listened. The disciples of science in the mid-century were many and credulous. The output of the press proved it. Great books

full of the new knowledge went through
large editions. Popular science lectures
were established in all the great centres.
The men of agnostic science went on tour.
They had crowded and enthusiastic audi-
ences. Their novel theories and speculations became the fashion of the hour in uni-
versities, in drawing rooms, and in workingmen's unions. Not to be able to talk Darwin and the Origin of Species was to be very
uninformed. Not to have at least dipped
into the hard and ponderous meditations of
Herbert Spencer was to be incompletely educated. Not to fall into praise of the classic
diction of Tyndall — not to be an admirer
of the bolder and more downright style of
his twin-star, Mr. Huxley, and not to know
at least the drift of their daring and sure
views, was to be a very old-fashioned person
and much "behind the times." Not to be
tinged a little with the crabbed, sour scorn
of Thomas Carlyle and gloat over the savage anger of the omniscient judgments he
chartered himself to pass on all mankind,
was to be unadvanced. Not to be tolerant
of Mr. Leslie Stephen in his open denial
and even flouting of the Divinity, or his
brother — one of the judges of England's
High Court of Justice — in his restless theological doubtings, was to be illiberal. To
speak disapprovingly of the mental gym-

nastics of James Anthony Froude in his
curious pilgrimage from Anglican monasti-
cism to the free shrine of the modern unbelief, was to undervalue true freedom of
mind. Such was the feeling which to a
very large extent prevailed in England and
the English-speaking world not so long
ago. There have been signs, too, that
similar motions of the scientific spirit had
taken place in most European countries.
Reviews of the foreign publications in Germany, France, Russia, Sweden, Belgium
and even Holland and Switzerland, made it
clear that this emancipation of human
thought from the trammels of the supernatural, was triumphantly proclaimed far
and near. In fact from the year 1850 to
the end of the next quarter of our century
the agnostic scientists had a fair and free
field. They had the reading multitude at
their feet. Men would listen now to no
other instructors, and great things were
vaguely hoped to come from the invigorat-
ing freedom of universal speculation. All
beliefs and traditions that hitherto prevailed
were to be put aside, and an entirely new
direction was to be given to thought and an
entirely different sort of knowledge to be
acquired. It appeared that this could not
be done without throwing discredit and
obloquy on the older order, and very bold

words were now said out loud, which formerly were suppressed for fear of coventry. "Oh, the freedom and the freshness of it," said one young man, who afterwards became quite famous, when he read for the first time that blaspheming enigma called *Sartor Resartus.**

No patient hearing could be gained for the literati of the old and orthodox side in all that time. Many were chary of criticising the new theories, lest they should be set down as opposed to learning and progress. And that was a terrible label to attach to one's self. A few prominent Catholic writers entered the list, but as a Frenchman finely says of them, it was only to carry on a *coquetterie réglée* with the scientists of skepticism. For, while guarding their orthodoxy by referring the ultimate cause of all things to the action of an omnipotent Creator, they freely embraced the theory of evolution, *i. e.*, the development by gradual process of everything and every one from identical germs.

With the best intention, no doubt, they made a sweeping sacrifice of the literal sense of Genesis, and wrenched somewhat violently the text of the story that men so long deemed sacred, as a concession to those

* See Mr. Huxley's obituary on Tyndall in "Nineteenth Century." February, 1894.

who were openly ignoring God, and denying all divine and supernatural action, in
the origin and growth of the world and its
denizens.

Now, evolution is not of such demonstra-
ble certainty that it does not leave us yet
free, to reject it if we choose, and while
giving all due credit to men of great ability
like Mr. Mivart and Mr. W. S. Lilly, we
may be permitted to question, whether all
their ingenious pains to set up an orthodox
evolution, have been repaid by any good
result.  They certainly made very little
impression on the agnostics, and their fel-
low-believers are not much more enlightened, while not a few may have suffered
from a disturbance of views to no useful
purpose.

There was one instance, however, of an
eminent lay-writer, whose steps were not so
mincing in the lists.   In a controversy with
the biggest man among the agnostics, in fact
the very inventor of that peculiar name —
agnostic — Mr. Gladstone held the old-fashioned language of an uncompromising Christian.   He spoke of  " Our Lord " and
" miracles "  and  " Satan"  and " divine
teaching " as a matter of course, without
the least show of human respect before
those mighty men of science.  It was edi-
fying to believers, to see this veteran of po-

litical strife make, at his great age, so brave
a stand for the supernatural, and though he
may have failed to convince his individual
antagonist, his sincerity extorted from Mr.
Huxley a handsome compliment at the close
of the argument; for he applied to the great
statesman the words invented by Shakespeare for Cleopatra : —

> " Age cannot wither him,
> Nor custom stale his infinite variety."*

But the day was coming, when a voice of
protest was to be raised, not from among
the believers, but from the ranks of the
friends and sympathizers with godless
science. These men of beliefless science were to be arraigned, and at length
asked to show, where was the benefit to their
fellow-men, from their theories so loudly
and confidently proclaimed. They were to
be summoned to point out what reliable
comfort they had built up, or were going to
build up, to take the place of the ancient
beliefs, that had been a protecting shelter
to men for ages long.

The public mind was more or less prepared, for this turn of events. People had
been awed, but had now grown a bit wearied

---

* See the "Nineteenth Century" — Gladstone-Huxley
Controversy on the miracle of the swine.

of the solemn, tiresome omniscience of these men, and so were in a mood to enjoy the revolt in their camp.

That pontiff of agnosticism — Prof. Huxley — shortly before his death (for alas! even so mighty a dictator in letters is not immune from the common lot of mortals) — composed a general preface, for the final reissue of his works. In this, he gives the public a bit of his early mental history, in his characteristic style. He says, that in the beginning of his scientific career, he found stretching across his path, and barring his way, the old traditions of revelation. They were regarded, as sacred and impassable. They were too high to climb, he tells us, and to crawl under them, he would not condescend—he disliked mud. In this dilemma, he bethought him of a third way to surmount the barrier. He would hew his way through, hack and demolish it! This he proceeded to do, and to his great relief, found it to be only lath and plaster and cardboard — mere rubbish! Having thus rid himself of the Bible, and all its tales, he marched unimpeded along his scientific pathway, with what practical results time, and his friends are beginning to show.

However, he was not summoned, from that happy pathway he had cleared for himself, before he was to witness, by an un-

pleasant irony, other and just as manly
hands as his, beginning to hack, and hew,
the barrier of scientific theories, which he
and his colleagues were at such pains to
erect, across the pathway lighted by faith.

The protest, which is beginning to be
heard, and which is quite a notable feature,
in the history of contemporary secular
thought, is not directed, it need scarce be
said, against scientists of that patient and
unassuming class, who do no hacking, and
hewing of sacred things. There are those,
who confine their scientific researches, solely
to the material benefit of their fellow-men.
Their laborious days have been given, to
smooth the rough places of life, and make
the human lot more bearable, through the
exceeding convenience of their ingenious
inventions, and marvelous discoveries. But
these men never cast disturbing trouble into
the souls of their fellow-men, nor sow dis-
quieting doubts, in human minds. Such
scientists are greatly, and deservedly hon-
ored. Watts, Stevenson, Thompson (Lord
Kelvin), Nasmyth, Pasteur, Quatrefages,
Virchow, these are the men, leaders of a
large and useful class, who are justly regarded, as benefactors of their kind. Any
one of these, is of more real worth to his
fellows, than all the monarchs, or states-
men, or great captains, who spent their

days amid the dire tragedies of human
slaughter, which fill so largely the history
of the race. There are few among living
men, who would not rather be a Pasteur
than an Alexander, or Napoleon, a Bismarck, or a Moltke.

It is not against scientists, such as these
that either complaint can be made, or reaction take place. The challenge, that is
now beginning to be delivered, concerns
only that class of scientists — biologists and
naturalists, who have pushed their work,
otherwise useful perhaps and lawful, beyond its legitimate limits, and assuming a
dictatorship over contemporary thought,
arrogantly demand, the surrender of all
previous beliefs, in favor of their scientific
researches — proposing these as the proper,
and only rational source of human knowledge.

Such a summons, issued in a tone of assured authority, has considerably disturbed
a multitude of minds, without adding anything to their happiness, and nothing whatever, to the hopes, that men will ever refuse
to relinquish.

The chief disturbers of the world's mental peace in our time, have been Hegel,
Schleiermacher, Strauss, Hartmann, Vache-
rot, Taine, Renan, Darwin, Tyndall, Spencer and Huxley — a formidable phalanx.

To these, on the literary side, must be
added the numerous theorists of the " social
question," who ignore the supernatural in
everything, that touches the human condition. Such are Karl Marx, Kropotkine,
John Morley, Carlyle, Hugo, Elisée Reclus,
Henry  George,  Louis  Blanc,  Leslie
Stephen, and the usual host of their imita-
tors in the public press.

As may be supposed, the religious leaders and teachers, have not been silent on
the side of belief. But such apologists, are
scarcely regarded at all, by those other men.
They are set aside, and superiorly despised.
Protests, merely professional, are not to be
taken seriously. They are Ciceronian
pleadings, *pro domo suâ*. In self-protec-
tion, such protests *have* to be made — a
mere matter of course, that everybody expects, and nobody minds. Interested witnesses, are out of court in this important
discussion, and so forth. The words of
professional religious teachers, gave no
alarm whatever to these agnostic scientists.
They treated them as something to be
amused at, or as a subject for their rail-
lery, and lofty scorn.

However, it was entirely another matter,
and much more serious, when murmurs of
misgiving and protest, began to be heard,
from the men behind them, from those,

whom they fully believed, to be sympathisers and supporters — from men, who lived far from the camp of the clericals.

Some few years ago, vague hints began to be heard, like stray shots, regarding the unsatisfying results of scientific conclusions, as the panacea for our mortal woes. A patient hearing had, hitherto, been given to the agnostic scientists, and men had been waiting in confident expectation, for their announcements. The magisterial tone of these eminent men of science had inspired— nay, imposed, that confidence.

In old times kings "touched for the evil." In our time — democracy, having exploded the divine in kings, and most other things— it was science that was to touch for the evils of humanity. But, now, that its magic hand had been, for some time, stretched forth to heal, it is not apparent that the evils of poor humanity are growing any lighter, or less. In fact, never before, have they been so pressed upon the public attention, or louder plaints uttered by the masses, as in our day. Science, it seems, has been "touching" in vain. In all its boasted pharmacopœia, there is no potent drug, for humanity's ills. And so, men, naturally, began to ask of the scientists, "What practical good, has come to the world from the years of your laborious researches — is a mere negative result, all we are to get for our patient waiting? ''

---

## CHAPTER II.

### Signs of the Reaction.

The first formulated, and, indeed, formidable complaint, came from a French academician, M. Ferdinand Brunetiére. This was a startling surprise, to the agnostic school, and caused a great sensation. He was not only a man of recognized eminence, in the literary world, but he always passed for a leader among Parisian *libres penseurs*. He published in the Review, of which he is the *Directeur-gérant* an article, treating of what, he very roundly and boldly called "the successive bankruptcies of science."

This article marks the date of the aggressive reaction against the scientists, of which we now see the rising tide.

Rénan, in his usual tone of tranquil confidence, had announced, that "religious beliefs will slowly disappear from the world, mined by primary instruction, and by the predominance of science, over literature, and education." Prof. Huxley wrote: "If the scientific method, working in the domain of history, philology, and archeology, has become so formidable to the dogmatic theologian, what may not be said of the scientific method, working in the domain of physical science?"

To them M. Brunetiére makes answer, not only in the article alluded to, but in others with which he followed it up in 1895, and 1896, that religious belief, far from disappearing, or being extinguished, by the "scientific method," is becoming recognized as the only basis of solution for the problem of man's social condition. In his interesting and able review of Mr. A. Balfour's book, "The Foundations of Belief" he says: "What is now discussed, is the question, whether *physically* or *physiologically* the necessity of belief, like the necessity of knowledge, must enter, in some part, into the very definition of man; whether *historically*, social evolution is conceivable without the supernatural, which has ever been mingled with it, as a guide and explanation; whether *morally*, it was ever possible to formulate a rule of conduct for men, which did not draw its sanction from the absolute."

He, thus, honestly forces on the attention of his scientific friends, the fact, that when men wish to analyze and account for humanity, from what point soever it may be looked

at, the "scientific method" is felt to be in-
sufficient, and that it is the religious
method (to borrow the word) which must
be relied on. M. Brunetiére ranges himself on this side, and freely admits that it
is as foolish, as it is futile, to banish the
supernatural from the discussion of the
grave problems of life. He is especially
strong on the impotence of reason, as the
only guide and sole source of knowledge,
and just as feeble as reason, science, its
hand-maid, has also proved to be. Science,
he asserts, has no answer to give to the
various social problems, which occupy pres-
ent-day thought so prominently; on that
account men are beginning to turn aside
from it, disappointed and dissatisfied, to
seek an answer somewhere else. Science
has been weighed in the balance of practical knowledge, and found wanting.

This, in substance, is the conclusion of
M. Brunetiére, and thus he bears witness,
that a real reaction has set in against
science as pursued by unbelievers. This
writer is a power in the French world of
letters. Unless his place were among the
foremost writers of France, he would not
be a member of her famous Academy. It
is easy, then, to imagine the dismay of his
fellow-agnostics, at such an avowal on his
part. Some of them called it the "great

betrayal." It was not that. It was only
the honest admission of his own return to
sound sense, in which he showed a great
courage in support of convictions unpop-
ular with his friends. It is a striking sign
of the times.

But in the world of English letters there
is another sign just as striking. At the
time that M. Brunetiére was confessing his
failure of faith in the "scientific method,"
another mind, not less trained and brilliant
than his, was engaged on the same line of
thought in England. Not long after the
Frenchman's declaration of the " successive
bankruptcies of science " in the *Revue des
Deux Mondes*, Mr. Balfour's thoughtful
book *"The Foundations of Belief"* fell, as
a surprise, on the world of London. It created a profound sensation. That so busy
a man, as the Leader of the Commons, could
find time for the lengthy and deep meditations, of which this book is the evidence
and expression, was astonishing enough.
But that one, whom high questions of State
are supposed to absorb, and whom the little
spiritualizing pursuit of politics chains to
utterly worldly things, should be discovered devoting a large share of attention to
the supernatural and the eternal questions,
was a shock to the worldly-minded and a
scandal to " advanced " thinkers of every

hue.  What gave special cause for uneasiness, was the great literary power and
charm displayed in the book.  It would
scarce be possible to treat in a finer and less
fatiguing vein, those grave questions, which
other writers of ability too often envelop
in metaphysical and unrefreshing obscurity.
There is a great variety in it, there is
novelty of view and originality.  There is
an easy and confidential tone — though lady-
readers, if it find any, may resent the bit on
bonnets, as decidedly rash for so confirmed
a bachelor as Mr. Balfour.  But you will
remark, besides, a grave earnestness in it,
which makes you feel that the author was
under the stress of the *liberare animam
meam.*

The whole drift of the book is, manifestly, a reaction against science of the
dogmatizing kind.  It is a plea for faith,
and a convincing call to reinstate the
supernatural in its own place as a source of
certitude and knowledge.  Twenty years
ago, the author, probably, would not have
had the courage to publish it, and if he had,
he would just as probably have got no
hearing on the subject.  His first book
bore the less open title of " *Philosophic
Doubt.*"  But the present one — a manifest invitation to believe — was the fashion
of the day and the book of the season.

This may be owing, in some measure, to the high place attained by the writer in the world of politics, but it is owing just as much to the fact that men's minds were prepared for it, and were feeling a want they find there, in part, supplied. It shows that thousands of others are thinking the same thoughts that Mr. Balfour has, so ably and so interestingly, put into words.

It is important to note, that a demand was at once made for a French translation of this book, and as a coincidence it is interesting to learn, that M. Brunetiére was asked to write its French preface. This shows how instinctively and quickly was recognized the identity of view between these two distinguished men, on the grave step of a return to religious thought — men who probably had never seen each other, lived in different countries, and had nothing in common, save their previous free-thinking tendencies. This is surely striking evidence of a reaction.

In my book, "*Disunion and Reunion*" I incurred no little criticism, and even ridicule, for the statement that Scotch people would yet wield an influence over English thought in the direction of the old faith. Mr. Balfour is a Scotchman !

M. Jules Payot, another of the French

*libres-penseurs*, in a book called "*De la Croyance*," enters his protest, also, against the shortcomings of science. Among other severe things he says: "My science does not hinder my ignorance of realities from being absolute; science has a symbolic language and an admirable system of signs, but the more it progresses, the farther it gets from the reality of things, and plunges into abstractions."

Mr. Benjamin Kidd, in his book, "*Social Evolution*," which has attained a wide and just popularity, also strongly expresses the same feeling of disappointment with the scientific method, and its exiguous results. This book of Mr. Kidd's has also had the honor of a French translation. This translation was made by M. Le Monier, and published by the firm of Guillaumin of Paris. This would seem to indicate a demand in France, just now, for a literature widely different from that of the old school of irreligious scoffers and incredulous philosophers.

There is scarcely any Review in Europe, or for that matter in all the world, which commands a greater influence among the literary public than the Paris *Revue des Deux Mondes*. So many of its contributors have, from time to time, been elected to the high honor of membership in the *Academie*

*Francaise*, that it has aptly been called the vestibule of that famous Olympia. Under the rule of its founder Mr. Buloz, it was unfortunately the happy hunting-ground of the most aggressive anti-religionists. It was through its pages M. Rénan first found an audience, and, for a long time, it remained merely the organ for agnostic free-thought. But of late it has come to its readers as a surprise to notice how it has been steadily veering round to the orthodox compass-point of religious thought.

Time was when this Review would not have published the following story of Count Cavour's end — even though written by the Count Benedetti: "In a lucid hour of his last illness Cavour sent for his servant — 'Martin,' said he, 'we must part. Send in time for Padre Jacobo, the parish priest of the Madonna dei Angeli; he promised to assist me in my last hour.' This priest was sent for and spent a half hour, hearing his confession. This he (Count Cavour) afterwards told to his friend Farini: 'My niece,' he said, 'has brought Father Jacobo to see me, for you know I must prepare for the great step into eternity. I have made my confession, later on I shall receive communion. I want all to know, especially I want the good people of Turin to know, that I die a Christian.'"

What! Cavour sent for a Catholic priest
and asked for the sacraments of the church?
What a scandal to the free-thinkers and
his fellow free-masons! Cavour, the noble
radical — the unrivaled statesman, whose
powerful mind swayed the councils of Europe, who was years ahead of his great co-
eval Bismarck in statecraft — the untiring
worker for Italia Unita — the intriguer with
the Carbonari and that plebeian bandit Gar-
ibaldi — the sworn foe of the Pope, and the
beloved of all devout Protestants — he send-
ing for a priest and dying an avowed Catholic — this should not have been made
known, it is such a bad example to the
atheistically enlightened! Yet it is in the
pages of the *Revue des Deux Mondes* for
October, 1896, that this piece of history
is given, vouched for by the distinguished
Ambassador who knew him well.

In the same pages too, has appeared far
the best appreciation of the life and work
of the late Cardinal Manning, from the pen
of a Protestant gentleman, M. Francis de
Pressensé. When his able and sympathetic
articles were published atterwards as a
book it was " crowned " by the French
Academy.

In this Review a writer of great and ver-
satile talent, with the liquid Bohemian
name of Wyzewa, is also permitted to give

a remarkable criticism of that stupendous work (in eight hundred and sixty-five parts) of the artist M. Tissot. The opening words of his critique are so much to the purpose of this chapter, that I may be pardoned for quoting them at some length in translation : " Every one has heard of that beautiful and good princess, who after long years of perfect wedded bliss was brought back by her husband and left in the wild woods where he first found her. Her only fault — truly a rare one — was that she was too good and too beautiful — at least so says the story. But I fancy, that born as she was in a wood, and knowing nothing but love, many little rustic traits helped to detach from her the princely husband's affections. Perchance he bethought him that she once tended sheep and was of rather low birth, or perhaps as he grew older he acquired new tastes and fresh desires, her natural disapproval of which he could ill brook. All we know is that he treated her most shamefully; but hardly had he again consigned her to her native woods than he was seen to run about the world in the most light-hearted manner looking for a more amiable princess and one worthier of being the wife of a prince like him, than the poor, discarded first love. He soon discovered, however, that the princess he had put away

was the best of them all; for none of those
he subsequently encountered could bestow
upon him the happiness he sought. So after
saying to himself twenty times over — no
doubt through pride or may be weakness —
that he never, never would recall her from
exile, still finding that he could neither live
nor die without her, he one fine day set out to
look for her again. The legend adds that
it was even a great happiness to him to have
succeeded in finding her, and though she
would have preferred his return grounded
on more tender reasons, such as deep regret
for his treatment of her and not merely
because he felt the want of her, she never-
theless, touched by his misery, forgot and
forgave. This is the only point where this
naive story falls short in perfect likeness to
another story that is *just now passing under
our eyes*. There is not one of the adventures of this prince that we can not compare
to our own adventures, since we banished
from our heart (some fifty years ago) the
old Christian faith that had been for so
many centuries our trusted and faithful
companion. . . . It had seemed to us
too childish, we grew tired of it, it interfered too much with our inclinations and we
too went about the world in search of a new
worship. Our hearts grew young in the
free air, and not a phantom rose before our

view but we decked it with all the graces.
First we adored science. This is what Rénan recommended us to do in exchange for
the faith he took from us. He set against
the ' unclean and puerile ideal,' he professed
to find in Christianity ' the superior sanctity
of the scientific ideal.' Science alone, he
said, was pure. But after forcing ourselves
to love the substitute, it was far from giving us the moral support we used to get
from Christianity. In fact we found it re-
fused us everything, even the smallest grain
of solid truth. Then, after how many
other specters did we run and found them
but phantoms that melted at our touch!
Like the prince in the story we were now
left alone, but just as little as he, were we
able to bear our solitude. For doing or
for dreaming — for living or dying we must
have a faith. This is why some of us have
taken courage, and have begun to deplore
aloud the loss of the old faith." A more
earnest testimony than this to the present
day reaction it would be hard indeed to find.

---

The popular reception given to M. Tissot's
marvelous artistic work in Paris, of which
M. Wyzewa writes with such sympathy in
the article from which the foregoing is
taken, is another very striking sign of this

reaction. This great artist has devoted ten
years of his life to the accomplishment of
this one work — no other than the painted
story of the life of Christ. He went out
to Palestine, as he himself tells us, with the
Gospel in his hand, and there studied on
the spot all the places where that divine
life was lived. The result of his work was
exhibited at the *Salon* of the Champ-de-
Mars in 1894. It forms a series of no less
than eight hundred and sixty-five different
studies.

It needed the courage of a great and sincere mind, thus to set once more before the
eyes of the most frivolous population in the
world, the entire life of our Savior. It was
also a strange venture, at this late date, to
handle again a subject exhausted by the
labors of so many others. Had it not been
treated a thousand times from every aspect
and had not the worldly-minded long since
turned weariedly away from it? Nothing
could possibly be thought of less inviting
to the mundane Parisians. Yet he never
faltered, and to leave no mistake about his
object, he appended to each painted scene
an explanatory note of his own, which confessed his faith and evidenced the reverent
spirit which prompted his work. His success was beyond all expectation. Seldom
has such a reception been given to any

artistic work in our time. For three
months, immense crowds invaded the gal-
leries in the Champ-de-Mars. Surprise,
respect, unstinted admiration were the
tribute paid to this supreme effort of Christian genius, and an eminent art critic, not
by any means of a pious turn himself, has
declared, that it was impossible for any one
who came there to leave without feeling
the better for having come and seen. This
splendid work seems like an inspiration.
It was completed about the time that
Ernest Rénan lay dying in Paris. He was
the Arch-Arian of the nineteenth century.
His cynical impudence in speaking of our
Lord was never surpassed. He called him
" that delicious young man from Galilee,"
and in another place " that delightful charlatan!" His treatment of the sacred life
had destroyed all idea of Christ's divinity
in thousands of minds. And now almost
at the door of his dying chamber, a reviv-
ing elixir was administered to the faith he
so powerfully strove to kill.

On the same lines, though in a different
way, the distinguished Russian writer, Count
Leo Tolstoi, has also been helping on the
reaction. That a layman of wealth, high
position, and scholarly attainments should

occupy himself in a serious and reverent
spirit, editing a version of the Gospel, at
this late hour of our era, is very disconcert-
ing to the Huxleyan minds that have so long
labored to discredit them. His book which
bears the title simply of " The Gospels "
was published in 1894 and in the following
year was translated into French.

In the introduction he declares at once
the motive of his writing, — " for me," he
says, " there is nothing at all so important
as this light which for eighteen hundred
years has illuminated mankind." He ex-
cuses himself from all discussion as to the
personality and history of Christ and he
adds — " it is enough for me that His doctrine is the only one that gives meaning to
my life."

---

It is also a significant fact, that in a very
recent number of a secular American magazine the Viscount Melchoir de Vogué, a
brilliant member of the French Academy,
should announce to the public of the United
States that, in his opinion, the greatest of
living men is the present Pope. And this
is not an *obiter dictum*, it is the thesis of the
article and in proof of this rather bold assertion he alleges that the Pope, as " an enlightened guide in the supernatural unto his

fellow-man, has been of more practical use
to them, and has afforded them more valuable help, than any of his contempo-
raries.''

As a psychological puzzle, I am tempted
to mention here a somewhat strange coincidence. While M. de Vogué was engaged
on this serious and evidently sincere piece
of work, which is also characterized by all
the thoroughness of his great ability, he was
at the same time, in another quarter, publishing a French story of a lubricious kind.
This story bears the title of "*Jean d'
Agréve*," and treats of a strange phase of
illicit love. It may, perhaps, be pleaded in
excuse, that the utter loathing created by
the vivid picture drawn of his hero as a
worthless, egotistic, self-pampered, uncleanly and sensual pagan coxcomb, and
by the no less repulsive picture of the heroine, as an utterly sensual married woman,
a mere animal in her sensuality, can not
but influence people in favor of the higher
and purer life — but he does not say so.
That is a risky way to inculcate virtue.

## CHAPTER III.

### What Provoked the Protest.

I think it is clear from the foregoing, that the reaction against the scientists, of the anti-supernatural and anti-religious class, has commenced and most likely will continue. It will be helpful to that end, and not without interest to many readers, to explain why people are dissatisfied with the researches of the agnostic scientists.

The reason is short and intelligible — their conclusions bring no comfort, and are of no use to any human mind in answering the questions that are always present to men — whence have I come, why am I here, and what is to become of me?

For instance :

The last question, personally and vitally, affects everybody. There is no more certain fact, than that we shall not be very long in existence here. What is going to happen then? Every individual human being wants to know something definite about that. The universal fact of death makes it so personally interesting to each and every one. Well, when the "scientific method" and its conclusions are eagerly scrutinized for information on this point of

such intense interest, people are amazed to
find, after all the parade made of them in
these recent years, that they are dumb on
this vital question. The utmost the hon-
ester scientists say is — We do not know.
Some less scrupulous say — There is nothing to follow or to happen. But that is
not honest for they give no proof — not the
shadow of a proof of their assertion.

The former, indeed, advise every one not
to trouble about it — to let themselves go
with the great tide of human life into the
void — the unknown. There is nothing to
fear, no cause for alarm. Now the great
mass of men never have believed, and' never
will believe that. It is no wonder their disappointment is great. An apt pupil of the
"scientific method" in her "Story of an
African Farm" declares, rather helplessly,
that "the tears of the mourners and the
mud of the grave cement the power of the
priests!" Rather halting logic in our
friend. One would think, it was the priests
invented death. They, poor men, have got
to face the muddy grave as well as other
people, and are quite as much interested as
to what is to become of them, as everybody
else, but they are not at all likely to be so
daring or reckless, as to lend themselves to
deceptions about a matter, that involves
their own outlook and well-being in com-

mon with all others.  This is a specimen of
predjudice-raising, which begets that daring
attitude in some, but which happily does
not satisfy the multitude.

---

But though the " scientific method " has
nothing to tell about the mysterious future
after death, it has a great deal to say about
our origin.

On this ground, science is much more at
home and very confident.  For, unlike the
future, the past at all events is real and ex-
plorable, and science claims it as its own
peculiar province for research.  For the
last forty years, lakes of ink and reams
of paper have been expended on reports
by the scientist of their independent search
across the ages for the first vital spark.
To prosecute their researches, quite un-
shackled by any preconceived notions, they
abolished and wiped out all previous maps
and charts, which used to serve humanity
as a guide over the distant and difficult
country of its past.  These maps and
charts they declared to be utterly useless
and misleading, and were accountable for
all the myths and superstitions about the
origin of mankind, which had so long de-
graded the human mind.  They would undertake this exploration anew, with com-

mon sense and enlightened reason aided by
the modern scientific method, as sole guides.
They would tramp every inch of that
ground to its utmost limits for themselves,
taking nothing from hearsay or tradition.
They would strip it of all its mysteries and
bogeys, and bring back but the plain, simple answers that honest nature had to give.
So they began, and ever since they have
led the world a lengthening and weary walk
through the domain of time.

At first the way was pleasant and interesting enough. It lay through the zoölog-
ical department of the earth. Here as long
as the study was confined to comparative
anatomy — the bone-structure of the various animal families, their similarities and
dissimilarities, it was curious and not unin-
teresting. Years of patient skill and labor
were devoted to this. To most people, the
motive of this minute curiosity about the
formation of the animal world, would have
been to admire the skill of the original de-
signer of those marvelous structures (in
which man had nothing whatever to do),
and be lost in wonder at the resources of his
great power. But the scientists never
stopped to call attention to that. *Their*
object was to find out what man really was
and how he came to be.

After more years of patient and minute

study of animal structure, a deliberate and
definite pronouncement was at length made
on the subject. Everybody now knows
what this pronouncement was, and with
what mingled feelings it was received by
the world when first put forth by Mr. Darwin. As the result of his long studies he declared, that man was not always as he is, that
he did not enjoy, as was hitherto supposed,
a distinct and different creation from the
animals, that he passed through other forms
before he attained his present shape, and in
a process which he called by the now famous
word *evolution*, man was shown to have
"descended" from the brute creation. He
even specified the immediate ancestor from
which, as far as his studies then warranted
him to say, he was gradually evolved in
the animal world. Many think Mr. Darwin
made a fatal mistake in thus particularizing,
for it was then the world laughed irrev-
erently, and theories that move to laughter
lose all their dignity. Though he clothed
his announcement in grave words of learned
sound — namely, that our dear ancestor
was *quadrumanous*, "arborial in his
habits" and *probably* (a concession, as he
was now to speak more plainly), "furnished
with a tail;" the facetious world caught the
meaning at once — "oh, we are descended
from monkeys — *et solvuntur risu!* That

was a severe check to the new biological
science and a poor reward for such long and
arduous labors.

But Mr. Darwin was quite serious, and
abated nothing in his arguments and his
assertions. His co-workers and followers
stood by him, and proclaimed his discovery a
triumph. But their investigations were not
going to end with our " quadrumanous "
friend, who was given to climbing trees
and was " probably furnished with a tail."

Arrived at this stage of man's existence,
the free investigators were only now, so to
speak, securely on the scent. They had
yet to arrive at the more elementary conditions of his earthly life. So, for many
more years, they wandered back through
the wastes of time. They searched the
rocks for fossils. They explored the caves,
and trawled the bed of the sea for specimens of life. They waded through swamps
and quagmires, and fished for tadpoles and
mud-fish. Then at last came the announcement that the utmost limit of primal living
forms had been reached. There in the
" cells " of those minutest creatures lay the
" fons et origo " of all terrestrial life. They
named it *protoplastic matter*.

From the mud-fish through varied forms
came all animals; and just the same as the
rest, from the mud-fish, through the ape,

came mankind! Not long since, Mr. Darwin's fellow-scientists and pupils erected a statue to his memory in his native town of Shrewsbury, Shropshire, England — presumably in gratitude for his elevating discovery as to their descent. "Hey! a mad world, my masters."

Since Darwin's time, further investigations have been made about this protoplastic matter. The scientists did not wish the world to suppose, that they knew nothing of its nature. They brought chemistry to bear on it. They took it into the laboratory, set out their crucibles, retorts, solvents and stills and worked out an analysis of this subtle substance — result; four gases, oxygen, hydrogen, nitrogen and carbon! By evolution, therefore, man, as we know him — "the thing to be demonstrated" of the scientists — was at one time a monkey, sometime previously — protoplasm, and prior to that, four gases! But the ordinary common sense of men will not be satisfied with these results. They do not account for man. They say nothing of his chief attributes. How is he, a thinking being, of great intelligence, capable of self-reflection, self-guidance and self-government? The agnostic scientists will not admit, that anything came to him from outside, as an endowment or the act of another being, their sole reason for not doing so, being the questionably logical one, that they have found no evidence of any creative act or creating being. A negative reason like this does not satisfy, as long as they are unable to supply a positive one, and assign a definite cause for a visible, palpable, undeniable fact, namely, *intelligent life*. It will not do to merely inform mankind, that aboriginally they were four gases. They inevitably want to know how the four gases came to think, to reflect, to make thought rule action and account to themselves for their sensations.

So for the practical minded, all those researches of the scientists into the origin of man and the sources of life, are entirely unsatisfying. They have failed to indicate any intelligible or adequate cause for composite human life, such as we all know it to be. They are dumb before the universally interesting question, which will never cease to be asked, Whence are we?

One of the most influential of those scientists — the man who gave the name agnostic to the sect (by no means new), not long before his death, made the bold, and what seemed to him, the consoling statement that "Christianity was driven to its last ditch." With gratitude the Christian may thank the man for teaching him that word. That

question — whence are we — is a final and
a fatal ditch for " science." Further efforts,
indeed, have been made to scramble out of
it.  Some relied on the theory of spontane-
ous generation, and elaborate experiments
were patiently made to sustain it.  But the
leading scientists honestly admitted that
this was not sustainable and, as is well
known, is now totally abandoned by the
scientific.  This conception of life, or the
living principle producing itself, involves a
mystery as great as any in the revelation,
which those scientists affect to discard.
Yet it was an unconscious adaptation of the
eternal begetting of the Word in the Godhead described by St. John.  But to trans-
fer what is, in the eternal and necessary
being, to the contingent and transitory, is
not in the rules of logic.

Others have since made a wilder, and
bolder plunge, to get out of the difficulty.
The appearance of initial life on this planet
they say is easily explained by the fact, that
the earth in its course through space encoun-
ters a lot of cosmic dust, which adheres to
it, and thus, mingled with this dust, living
germs of protoplastic, thinking matter
found a home on our globe.  But this ingenious theory is as little final as the others,
for where or when in cosmic space did this
living protoplasm get its life, and how came

it to be endowed with the wonderful poten-
tialities, of which the mental and physical
faculties of men and women are the development? That will not do.

Thus the labors of unaided science have
failed to give us any light on the question
which so personally interests every living
human being — Whence are we?

—————

There is another question just as pressing,
and more important to men, on which the
independent scientists, according to their
engagement, are bound to satisfy them —
Why are we here at all?

Their investigation of this question — the
*purpose* of human life — has not resulted in
anything pleasanter and more encouraging
for us than their dissertations on our origin.

In Mr. Darwin's books the "*Descent of
Man*" and "*The Origin of Species*," as
well as in the writings of those who follow
and indorse him, all we learn is, that mankind has been cast into the melée of this
world — to fight! to struggle for his very
existence, and in that struggle to prove his
fitness to live by "surviving."

I do not think it exaggeration to say,
that this is absolutely all that can be learned
from those bulky volumes on the vital
question — Why are men here at all?

When you come to extract from those
books any practical or serviceable meaning
or conclusions, the only wonderful thing
left you to admire, is that men could write
so much and say so little.  But when their
conclusion is arrived at, it is only vexation
of spirit.  Of what use or comfort is it to
humanity to be told, that there is a com-
pelling and invariable law of struggle in
animated nature, in which the weak must
always go down before the strong — the
ill-suited yield to the " fittest."   For whose
particular amusement this rather savage
game was invented, or to what use the sur-
vivors were to put their " survival," these
writers do not seem to have any sort of
care.   Why, a prize-ring has more meaning
than the theater of human life, in their
view.   Not to seem entirely barren, however, in their speculations, those ignorers
of a divine purpose apply evolution to man
in his " survived " stage.   He is not by
any means done with evolution after merely
surviving.   That is a slow, majestic, if
despotic, process, which is never more to
let go its grip.   Formed into society as a
survived species, man must go on evolut-
ing, constantly tending to a state of greater
perfectability and so *ad infinitum.*   That
may be all very well for the individuals of
the race who may reach that end, but what

about those who have passed off the scene,
those who are passing now, and who will
daily pass off through " death's cruel gate,"
before tasting the delights of this vague
perfectability of the scientists. Truly a
vexation of spirit. And that is all they
have to say. And if asked whether the
deeds, done in the days of his surviving,
have any bearing personally and as an individual on man's condition after he dies,
or what is to become of him then — they
say, " Oh, we are agnostics; you must not
ask us anything about these mysterious
things; we do not know, for science has
*told* us we can not know anything about
them. Science has not discovered any intelligent Creator, nor any meaning in life,
beyond a struggle for existence, never came
across such a thing as a soul, nor discovered
any trace of any other existence or world
for man but this." This is the last word
of science, so turn down the lights, the
lecture is over, and the audience is left
groping and bumping against each other
in the dark.

These unsatisfying results of agnostic
science have provoked the protest of which
we saw the clear indications in the preceding
chapter, and most people will allow that it
was time, for the credit of common sense,
to protest.

## CHAPTER IV.

### Agnostic Socialism.

The frequent failure of the "scientific method" applied to the condition of life, is another reason for the reaction. The scientific method of course makes a *tabula rasa* of all previous religious traditions. Religion, that is, a knowledge of supernatural things and their relation to us, science has declared unproven. It is, therefore, to be set aside, and not taken into account, in the problems of man's conduct and existence.

When men, then, in our time, came to think, on account of the great inequality of fortune and increase of want, that society should be reconstructed, or at least readjusted — many schemes were proposed for this end. Most of them proceeded on agnostic lines, that is, were purely materialist and secular, and omitted all calculation on man's spiritual nature, its demands, its defects and its aspirations. A fair type of these proposals is to be found in Mr. Bellamy's book, "*Looking Backward*." He did well to lay the scene of it in the year 2000, when none of his readers will be there to enjoy the delightful happiness of his reconstructed society. However, we have the advantage of

4

having witnessed some experiments in this reconstruction so brilliantly depicted *on paper*. It will be interesting and conclusive to give the story of a few of them.

In 1894, in the city of Brisbane, Queensland, a lame printer, named Lane, assumed a mission to his fellow-trademen and laborers, inviting their co-operation for a new social scheme. He had long been known as a labor organizer, and a leader in the unions. But nearly all the strikes he had engaged in, and helped on so actively, had ended badly in the long run for the workers.

This led him to think it was impossible to improve the social conditions of the workingman, while surrounded by the class prejudices and the adverse influences of the wealthy in society as at present constituted. Suppose they could be moved away from those surroundings and, putting oceans between them and those irritating, stupid class divisions, and given a chance to found society anew on the lines laid down by the clever theorists he had long studied and admired, there was no reason why they should not succeed.

It was a poor compliment to the Queensland government, whose legislation in favor of the workingman had for some time been notorious, and by some people deemed far too socialist and radical. But it failed to satisfy the aspirations of Mr. Lane and his friends. He drew up an outline of his project, and addressed it not only to the workingmen of Queensland, but also to the workingmen of all the Australian colonies. As many as could contribute a little to a common fund necessary to start them (I think it was £60), were invited to come away to Paraguay in South America, and found a New Australia. Nor was this a step in the dark, for Lane had been in communication with Paraguayan authorities who, anxious for immigration and too poor to pay for it, like its richer neighbors of the Argentina, welcomed his proposals and offered grants of land in the interior. This was a great inducement, but a greater was the perfect freedom they were to enjoy. No clergyman or preacher of any kind was to be allowed to join. They were to have no church or profess any religion. No lawyers were to come — they should have no courts nor police. Community of interests, and as much as possible community of goods, was to secure agreement and exclusion of all class distinction, and guarantee good fellowship and happiness. Well-ordered industry, without the slavery and stigma of labor, would insure prosperity without the unnecessary abundance which

had bred the luxury and idleness so cor-
rupting and baneful to the old society.

Hundreds of applications poured in.
The money was freely deposited. Lane
chartered a large sailing vessel and had her
laden (in Sydney harbor) with provisions
and implements requisite for pioneering.
So numerous had been the applications that
all could not be accommodated on the first
voyage. A selection of about 300 was
made, and in due time with a great flourish
from the labor world, and an ovation from
the unemployed, in which Sydney seems
always to abound, they set sail for their
New Australia beyond the wide Pacific.

It is a weary way round the Horn to the
La Plata, and from the banks of that famous river to the site of the New Australia
it is a long trek, as they say in Africa. So
those of us, who felt an interest in watching
the result of this extraordinary modern
socialist experiment, had to possess our
souls in patience when the good ship was lost
to view. It was undoubtedly a remarkable event in our times, and full of interest
for every one who gave a thought to the
great social problem. Those men had gone
out to teach the world a realistic lesson in
building up the proper kind of human society. They would put to a practical test
the favorite paper social theories that of

late had got such wide circulation. The world had reason to feel obliged to them. A valuable wisdom was to be learned from the result.

Nearly a year went before we had any tidings. Lane's first report of things was favorable enough. All had arrived in safety. The Paraguayan Government had been as good as its word and besides had been very helpful. There was just a hint that great difficulties had to be overcome, there were many things which could not be foreseen nor provided for beforehand. Still it was too soon to be either too sanguine or discouraged. Meanwhile he recommended that the applicants, who could not be accommodated on the first trip, should now be forwarded with fresh supplies, and he promised that the newcomers should find everything in good shape and should not have to contend with the discomforts of first settlement.

(By the way, the lands of one of the old Jesuit missions once so famous and flourishing in that distant land had been assigned them.) On this report two hundred more, if I rightly remember, set out on the second expedition.

They were not very long gone, when a rumor from another source reached the Sydney press that things were not going

smoothly in Lane's Utopia, with a caution
to other intending emigrants to await
further developments. This caused some
uneasiness, and the news of the arrival of
the vessel in the Plata was anxiously looked
for. It came. At Monte Video the new
emigrants were surprised to find some members of the first expedition waiting for
them. No, they had not come to greet
them and show them the way — they were
waiting for a chance to get back! Alas!
poor humanity; it was the old story — dis-
agreements, disputes, jealousies, schism.
The thing was not working, they said, and
was not going to work. Lane was a dictator.
They fancied they had come out to be rid
of that kind of thing, but they were
deceived, and so on.

Having come so far and the complainants
being comparatively few, the second batch
continued on their way to see for themselves.

There was silence again for another inter-
val on the subject in Sydney. Then more
rumors found their way into the papers
from time to time. Now it was an interview
with a returned New Australian, again it
was a defense from Lane and explanations
from his friends, then recriminations until
people did not know what to think. After
a while came a consular report that distress

was prevailing among the immigrants; that many had found their way to the coast, were destitute among a people whose language was not theirs, and were begging passages home in English ships!

Last scene in this eventful history: A member of the New South Wales Parliament unfolded to the House so dismal a story of the plight in which these New Australians found themselves, so far away in a foreign land, that a motion for their relief was generously carried, and measures were sanctioned to facilitate their return home. So ended this scheme to reconstruct society on the sciencific method of ignoring all knowledge of man's first beginning or last end. The promoters forgot one all-important matter, that whoever would reconstruct society, where it needs reconstruction, should first reconstruct *human nature.* And science has nothing to say about that.

---

The second case is still more instructive, for this second attempt at solving the social trouble, was backed by all the resources of well-ordered government and legislative authority. It had none of the drawbacks of emigration nor the heart-breaks of dis-

tant exile.  It was carried out comfortably
at home.

There is no place in the world where secular socialism, that is, a socialism without
any reference to God, man's relation to his
will or laws, conscience or any supernatural
consideration whatsoever, has had so fair a
field or so much in its favor as in the
Australian Colonies.  Universal suffrage,
which, in one of them at least, includes
women, has given the making of the laws
into the hands of the so-called common people, because in a new country the common
people are for a long time in the immense
majority.  The policy of the governors sent
from England is, as far as I have seen, not
to interfere with any domestic legislative
arrangements which the colonists see fit to
make.  This legislation, notably in Queensland, South Australia and New Zealand, is
inspired by all the modern secularist social
doctrines.  Equalization of wealth, leveling
class distinctions, expropriation of large
landholders, the land for the people, re-
sumption by government of public convey-
ance, telegraphic and telephonic service
(an immense source of patronage) public
funds to be advanced to the people for
private enterprise, chiefly agricultural however, easy marriage laws and facilities for
divorce, free, secular, and compulsory edu-

cation, perfect independence in voting, no
privilege on account of class or calling,
accorded by the State — such is the programme. Surely never before had the
"people" such a chance to realize their
dreams of prosperity and social happiness. Let us see how much of that they
have attained. Ten years ought to yield
results enough to judge by, and that is
about the time the Legislatures have been
cleared of the old conservative, exclusive
and aristocratic control. I shall take the
Colony with which I am best acquainted —
New Zealand. In 1896 there were more
prisoners in the immense jails of Auckland,
Wellington, Christchurch, and Dunedin
than in 1886. The four large asylums for
the insane were overcrowded in 1896, the
smallest accommodating five or six hundred
patients. In 1893, the most dangerous
and damaging labor strikes brought trade
almost to a standstill, and caused much
privation and suffering. These few facts
speak for themselves. Popular legislation,
so far, left humanity pretty much as it found
it, perhaps a trifle worse. Yet " labor members " were numerous in the legislative Assembly; into the Council or *Upper House*
were introduced four journeymen, a boiler-
maker, a printer, a compositor and a joiner,
while among the Ministers, the real rulers

of the country, were an ex-pedler and ex-
miner and "pub" proprietor (these two
became Prime Ministers) and ex-grocer and
a telegraph clerk!

Their greatest experiment in social equality and an approach to orderly communism
was the founding of *Village Settlements*.
This scheme originated in New Zealand and
was adopted later in some of the Australian
Colonies.  It was a plain attempt to give
reality to Mr. Bellamy's prophetic visions and
therefore interesting to follow its fortunes.

The chief features of the scheme were
these : —

Associations were to be formed consist-
ing of not less than twenty persons.

To each member of the association the
government would allot sixty-four acres of
land and a money loan of fifty pounds to
be repaid at five pounds a year for ten years.
Five pounds an acre should be spent each
year on improvements.  Every association
was to be directed by a board of three trustees, elected by the villagers from their own
body.  No member should have any private
or separate interest in the land, save the
possession and use of that portion allotted
to him by the Trustees.

The rules of living and work were very
minute.  They provided for the kind of
members to be admitted.

Women were eligible. Asiatics were not. No member was to be admitted without the sanction of the board. The board had power to expel members for disobedience to rule, or absence from work without leave. An appeal lay from the board's decisions to the body of the members, who decided by vote — a bare majority sufficing. The board resumed possession of the rights of the expelled, and even of the deceased, realloting the property for the benefit of the community. The board was elected for one year, and was eligible for re-election. The board's powers were very extensive. They were what Fourier, that patriarch of Socialism in France, three-quarters of a century ago, imagined they ought to be. Probably the promoters of that Parliamentary Bill at the antipodes, had made acquaintance with the views of that fertile dreamer. The board was charged with the responsibility of the villagers to the government. They regulated the work to be performed, assigned to each one his task and prescribed the hours. The board managed the co-operative stores, and fixed the payment-in-kind to be made to each family — money currency was to be dispensed with. The functions of mayor, corporation and magistrate were discharged by the board and they were besides constituted inspectors of domestic arrangements and guardians of the general welfare — in fact such a *Pooh-Bah* was never seen as this board of the Village Settlement.

As regards the earnings, it was arranged that two-thirds were to be distributed as dividends, the other third reserved for interest and improvements. Any one incapacitated from work, without fault, would continue to participate to the full share in results.

The villagers were to show deference and respect to the members of the board. Residence was compulsory. All absences should be duly authorized, save a half-month's holiday in the year, which was a right. No buying or selling was to be permitted in the settlement without the knowledge and sanction of the board. If the board ordered the profits made by any individual whether within or without the association to be paid into the common fund, it should be done. All tools and implements were to be looked on as the property of the community. All were to consider themselves as possessing only the use of the land and not proprietors or farmers in the old sense. Every Friday dockets or coupons were to be distributed to each family entitling the bearer to supplies of all kinds at the stores. Finally, the legal dissolution of the association could be declared by the "general assembly" of all the members — but not before the State was safe-guarded in all its outlay and all debts paid.

Such were the Village Settlements in New Zealand and other Antipodean regions — praiseworthy effort no doubt to advance the well-being of the people. It is sad to relate they have all been dismal failures, and the reason is not far to seek.

It would be very blamable to make it a reproach to the promoters who now wield the political power, that they once were peddlers, publicans or petty clerks. But it is a reproach to these men, that they gave the bad example to the people they professed to serve, of discarding all religion from their own lives and excluding all consideration of its restraining influences over men, from their management of public affairs. A late workingman Prime Minister in New Zealand, was once notorious as a lecturer on the atheistic platform and when he came to die — cut off in his prime — the whole country knew that to the end he was true to his principles and false to his God. He was buried with civil rites. In those days when that two-handed fallacy and most fallacious of shibboleths — *liberty of conscience* — is bandied about. it may be said that no one should find fault with a man's opinions or professions. But in the ordinances of God and in the matter of obedience to His will who can honestly pretend there is liberty of "conscience" or conduct for anybody? And if men assume that there is no God to be taken into account, nor any rules laid down by Him for human conduct, the logic of facts quickly refutes their assumption. The failure of agnostic Socialist schemes such as the Colonial Village Settlements demonstrates that unless men feel themselves answerable to a higher and greater power than their fellow-men, and amenable to a Judge whose reprimand and award reach far beyond this life, they never will be capable of the self-sacrifice, self-restraint and self-denial absolutely necessary for living or laboring together with any approach to peace and concord.

So after but a few years of trial, most of those Village Settlements have broken up. Quarrels and bickerings, in some cases accompanied by assault and violence, were reported from all sides until the governments are pretty sick of their experiments.

In South Australia towards the end of 1895 it became necessary to institute a parliamentary inquiry into the state of those Village Settlements. Thirteen such associa-

tions had been there established but two
years before. The evidence given before
the committee was deplorable and conclusive. The settlers were found to have
fallen into debt all round, to the government, to merchants, to the banks. The ,
Board charged settlers with idleness and
incapacity, the settlers charged the Board
with despotism. In some of the villages
with not more than two hundred or three
hundred inhabitants, distinct parties had
already been formed, as inveterate in opposition as any Tory to Whig or Radical to
Liberal-Unionist. Alas! poor humanity.
Another strange feature appeared. Nearly
all the settlers, before they entered the
association, were ardent disciples of the
lectures under the " red flag " and readers
of the abounding communistic press. The
Village Settlement was the beau ideal of
these theorists — the practical reality of
their doctrines. A short trial brought a
rude undeceiving. One man was heard to
declare that for years he had been an advocate of " the land for the people" — but
now he preferred to believe in " the land for
Tom O'Grady " without " the people."
Another had been eager to live where every
one was to be a brother and sister, but now
he thought it more peaceable to be a friendless orphan, and so on. They all agreed

the Conservative party, which for some
time has been in a hopeless minority.
Like the Tories in England who fell back
on the rump of the dissident Liberals
and became Liberal-Unionists in order to remain in power, the Conservatives were ready
to ally themselves with any old party that
would give them a chance of a majority.
They adopted the platform of the liquor Pro-
hibitionists — with somewhat wry faces it
may be supposed. They also gained some
strength from those, and they were many,
whose confidence was shaken by some recent
financial blundering of the popular party's
ministry. But to no avail. They were
defeated at the polls, and those important
expiring leases are at the discretion of the
land nationalizers.

But it was not alone for renewed leases
the large land-holders were fighting, it was
for their very existence, for there was yet
another land measure passed by the Popular
party which affected them most seriously.
It was the "progressive land tax" bill,
which provides that taxes shall go on increasing in heavier and heavier ratio on
every thousand acres of pastoral land above
the prescribed number of acres. It is
another way of expropriating the big land-
owners. Coming, together with the large
outlay necessitated by the rabbit-pest, it

has made large station owning a losing and
ruinous occupation. Some proprietors have
already sold out to the government, the
only available customer, and all would be
willing to do so and leave the country if
they could. Thus the workingman's government will be ultimately free to parcel out
the land among the workingmen. The
outcome of this very courageous legislation
cannot of course be fully foreseen, for it is
only the next generation will be witness of
final results. But one experiment already
made by the government, with an estate
purchased from dissatisfied owners, does
not augur fair things for their further ven-
tures in the future. It is now widely
rumored that the government has not found
the State farmers of this *Cheviot Estate*
any less troublesome, more honest or hap-
pier than the village settlers. The truth
is, those new legislative reformers of
humanity are attempting the impossible
task of promoting the contentment and
happiness of men, without improving that
human nature from which all their miseries
spring. The genius of the "scientific
method," which entirely ignores the cultiva-
tion and correction of that human nature,
is deluding these obstinate but well-mean-
ing politicians of agnostic socialism. A
whole generation has now issued from the

free and secular schools founded also by them. And what result can be looked for from pupils, who never once, within their walls, had heard inculcated the only effective principle of moral restraint and self-control, nor ever heard mentioned the name or existence of the supreme Arbiter of human conduct? In some schools indeed such things have been mentioned — only however to be sneered at by the atheist teachers, of whom there are a very large number in these State schools. The evidences accumulating from every side of perverse and vicious conduct, demonstrate the utter inability of those purely secular experiments in Socialism to meet the aspirations of humanity for a more tolerable mundane existence. No wonder people are beginning to clamor for some more successful solution.

It will be well worth while then, in the next chapter, to show that this very socialism and communism so much advocated in these latter days, and so often abortively attempted by some men, are not only not impossible and unattainable, but have for centuries been realized and actually exist, with the happiest results in the world of to-day.

## CHAPTER V.

### Instances of Real Socialism.

There is in the world at this present moment a body of men, numbering roughly some twelve thousand associates. They are drawn, in most part, from the poorer classes. They are strangers to each other in the sense that they come not from the same place or even from the same country— they are of many nations. There is no distinction of rank or class among them, save what good order requires. The places of authority are filled by election and, in the minor trusts, by appointment. All, whether in authority or not, are equal before the general regulations or rule of life. They possess property, places of abode and means of subsistence, but everything is *in common*. No individual possesses anything in his own right, yet all have the use of what is owned. They may inherit from relatives and others as individuals, but such inheritance may be used only for some good purpose and by permission. They can, however, will it back to whom they please outside their own body. They work, not as they please, but only as work is assigned them. The main employ-

ment is of one kind, they teach, mostly the
poor. They teach too those who can pay,
to be able to teach more of the poor who
can not. They also instruct the ignorant
of the adult working classes. After that,
they do all their own domestic work. Beyond the marketing and cooking and clean-
ing up, that is very little, each one in his
private life being his own servant. They
are ready, however, at all times, for any
deed of neighborly benevolence that may
lie at their hands to do. They have joined
the ambulances in time of war. They have
their own times for relaxation and moderate
enjoyment, but the pleasures which the
world pursues, with so much zest and cost,
concern them not. They are never permitted to be unoccupied. Their day is of
seventeen hours and minutely regulated.
Their night is of seven hours from 9 p. m.
to 4 a. m. or 10 p. m. to 5 a. m. in some
climates. They are not lovers of the soft
life. They live together in groups and call
each other "brothers." They are inter-
changeable from group to group, and
though they are scattered widely through
the world, all follow one and the same rule
and obey one voice. At stated times they
hold general assemblies, each house electing a representative delegate. They have
thus existed for over two hundred years.

They join young, live long, and die in the
ranks. They renew the dead by ever increasing volunteers. In sickness and old
age they receive a constant and tender care.
They must needs like this life, and must
deem it happiest and best for them, to abide
in it so long. This is a living and wonderful fact for all men to see.

---

Again, there is a body of women in the
world to-day, numbering some fourteen
thousand. They differ from the men, just
alluded to, in that they are drawn from all
classes of society, from families of wealth
and title, down to the daughters of the poor.
They differ too, in that their works have a
range as wide as human wants. They tend
leper hospitals, or smallpox patients, or yellow fever cases. They teach fashionable
academies or instruct little dusky natives under tropical skies. They go under fire on
the battle-field to aid the wounded, or into
the slums of towns to dress the sores of the
uncleanly sick, and charm away, by sooth-
ing words, the sullen despair of the suffering poor. They give lessons in painting,
lectures on physical science, or preside at
an organ. They cook like professional
*chefs*, wash the pans and kettles, launder

and scrub the house. They train the workman's child to lacemaking and embroidery, short-hand, and typewriting, or take charge of a lunatic asylum or a female prison. They have open homes for the friendless young of their sex, and shelters, with a sister's welcome, for the fallen and unfortunate, — fourteen thousand of them, busy ever, at all these works all over the world! And all that work they do for nothing. There is no personal gain — they get no money for it, individually. There is no rank or division of class among them. The countess and the peasant work side by side. They wear the same costume — the same plain and rather coarse garb. You can scarce tell who is who, for all are trained to gentle manners, and when they want to spend a few pennies they often laugh together to find they have not got them. Though they have gone apart from their own kin to live with strangers, they have homes in common wherever they go and they call each other " sister," which they truly are to each other in will and deed. They rise at 4 o'clock at all seasons and in every climate, and there is scarcely a climate where they are not found, and they retire at 9 p. m. Through their long day, they agree to be busy, always busy. They agree to be cheerful too, to help others

through sorrow. Their government, or
plan of management, is very simple but
very perfect. They are all subject to one
head, and that is a man. He is called the
director. But he is not absolute or despotic.
There are others to whom he is responsible,
and he guides only by long-established rule.
There is ample and full protection for the
weakest and youngest among them. Brave
and wonderful little army! Death claims
them as other mortals, but their ranks never
seem to thin. Human hearts beat beneath
their blue serge robe — women's hearts,
with all a woman's tenderness and yearnings — but disciplined. They, too, have
their general assemblies now and again,
and then it is wonderful to hear them tell
the blended story of their world-wide
experience; for the great human drama
has been unfolded before them in the
by-ways of life — the fierce passions at
play, the hopes, the fears, the griefs,
and joys of the human struggle — they
have witnessed it all, and borne part in
the action.

Among themselves they are republican
simplicity and equality, and if one is given
charge, as must needs be, she is obliged to
call herself *the servant*, to obviate distress-
ing airs, and keep her humble. For women
are prone, perhaps more so than men, to

men's great weakness, which Shakespeare
so finely censures —

> " Man, proud man,
> Clothed in a little brief authority,
> Doth play such tricks before high heaven
> As make the a   els weep,"

or laugh perhaps would be better. They
are guarded against that, and are not permitted to distress each other, or either
amuse or grieve the angels. They choose
never to call anything their own — they say
*our* shoes, and if things get mixed in the
washing they do not mind, provided they
fit when théy put them on. They sit at the
same table and eat the same food, what one
has, all have. What could be more perfect
*communism* than this? Have you ever
heard of *socialism* more complete? Nor is
this a state of things they are merely ex-
perimenting on. Their association came
into existence about the time that London
was burning and was made desolate by its
great plague. And for these two centuries
and more, without dispute or quarrel, this
same life has been lived by multitudes of
those weak and gentle women. They must
have found it good to live so. The stage
of experiment is over long ago, and at this
hour, there are some fourteen thousand who

live so still, and make no noise about it
either.

———

There is yet another body existing in our
time, who have gone apart from their kind-
red, to live a similar life in their own fashion.
It is again, a body of men. I have lately seen
it stated, that, at the present moment, they
number about fifteen thousand. They differ
from the former bodies, in that they are
drawn from the aristocracy of talent. Except a minority of lay-associates, who do the
lower order of work, but who yet enjoy to the
full, equality of membership, and share in
the common life; all the rest are gentle-
men highly educated and accomplished.
This element is admittedly the hardest to
deal with in the matter of socialism, for
"knowledge puffeth up," as a wise writer
said long ago — and nothing puffs up like
it. Yet three hundred and forty years
have gone by, since they first came together, and without any friction from
within, they have succeeded in merging self
in the common number, and have lived in
true fraternity, equality and that liberty
they like best. No matter how much the
general body gains in wealth, or acquires in
property, it does not make any individual
among them one doit or dime the richer.

No member wants or cares to own anything, not even the coat or hat he may be
wearing, and were he asked to take them
off, and let another have them, he would
do so and receive others though inferior.
There are no parties among them, nor any
private enterprise or interest to be pursued.
All yield themselves voluntarily to the
strictest discipline, and each receives his
orders what to do or where to go, even to
the most distant place, without a murmur.
They have common homes and a common
table, and like the others only seven hours'
rest. Their employments are very varied,
but their main work is secondary and higher
grade teaching — next to *having* knowledge, is the pleasure of imparting it, and
the years are long that they devote to its
acquisition. However there is this pecu-
liarity in their institute. After the general
and thorough training, to which all are
submitted, has been completed, then great
latitude is allowed to individual bents and
tastes. One man has a taste for oratory —
well, an orator let him be, and give him all
the time, that the drudgery and toil of
oratory require.

Another man likes astronomy — they
build him an observatory, and stock it with
instruments. They have three very famous observatories at present, at Rome,

Manila, and Havana. They will let their
man go in charge of government as-
tronomical expeditions. One died at the
Cape in such employment not long ago.

Another man has a talent for writing —
let him write by all means, and have every
facility for publication. Or they found a
monthly magazine and let him edit it.

Another loves teaching — they find him
" a chair " and make him a life-long professor.

Another thinks he can manage the
strange peoples of distant countries — they
send him to China, Korea, and Japan.

Another has a tact for civilizing savages ;
they plant him among the very worst specimens to be found, in Northwest Australia
and Borneo.

Another has the social gift, and will carry
weight in society ; they give him a good
coat and let him dine out.

Another has a turn for the physical sciences — they build him a laboratory, supply
him with chemicals and a microscope, and
let him correspond with "learned societies."

Thus the widest room is given to individ-
uality, yet from one governing hand go out
the threads of the wide network, that holds
all in the unity of the common life.
Whenever and from wheresoever they are
called back, they come. Wherever sent,

the courage of sincerity. It all reads like
some   far-off,   old   religious   romance,
rather than a true story of real life from
our worldliest of centuries.

But the strangest and saddest part of
it is the singular choice he made of a guide
to that hard and mystic way. This was
a certain American, an ardent preacher of
the higher life, and the better way. It
is almost unaccountable, how a man of
Oliphant's intelligence and worldly experience, should have fallen so easily under the
influence of that person, who, as the sequel
showed, was more of an adventurer, if not
a mountebank, than a spiritual enthusiast.
Yet so it was, even to the extent of utter
self-abandonment. He and his young
wife accompanied him to America, and
having made over to him all their money,
and even their personal effects, were put
to work by him on his communistic farm.
His despotism over them went the length,
not only of imposing the rudest and most
drudging toil upon those refined people,
but of separating them, and forbidding
them even to speak to each other. But
their fortitude soon gave way, and they
came out of this painful and humiliating
experience, shattered in health and fortune,
and survived it only a very few years.

On the other hand, the thousands of people, banded together under similar conditions, in the three associations I have described, succeed and persevere unto the end, happy in their undertaking.

That description is no fancy sketch.

These associations are living facts visible before the world and have names. The first is an Order of French origin known as the Brothers of the Christian Schools, commonly called in English " The Christian Brothers." The second, also of French foundation, is the congregation of the " Filles de la Charité " — the famous Sisters of Charity — those with the great, white, wing-like bonnets supposed to be adapted from the Picardy or Norman peasant head-dress of the seventeenth century. And the third is the celebrated Order whose members write the formidable S. J. after their names — Societas Jesu — Jesuits.

One of the moral wonders of the world is the Noviciate of the Sisters of Charity in the Rue du Bac, in Paris; touching on the wicked Latin quarter, the *seminaire*, as they call it, seminarium, in spiritual botany, the nursery, where the seeds of piety in every variety are planted under cover, and its tender shoots sprout in warm shelter from passion's storms. If you are respectable, and get yourself authenticated you can have a peep. Under an old portico in

that rather dingy street, you enter one of
the largest private properties in the heart
of that great city. When I saw the Novi-
ces, it was on a procession day. They
numbered, then, between five and six hundred. It was a wonderful sight. The
bloom of youth was on them all — and
beauty's bloom on many — the usual slender proportion of it, as in any crowd of the
sex. They were dressed all alike — half
cap, half old-fashioned bonnet — a fichu
and plain black gown — like decent, cleanly, French country girls. They were of
many nationalities — of all ranks. The
neighboring, aristocratic Faubourg St.
Germain, was even represented. It was
delightful to hear that immense chorus of
young voices in the hymns. What a holo-
caust to heaven in those young lives.
They were here preparing, in innocence and
purity of life, for the great renouncement.
Out from that training cot, would go those
carrier-doves of the Divine Compassion, to
minister to all humanity's miseries. For
two hundred years they have been going,
into every clime, across many seas. They
are going still, if indeed, they have not
been evicted by those noble persecutors of
all that is good, messieurs the municipal
councillors of Paris.

A little farther down on the same " Rive

Gauche," near the "Invalides," you may
see a similar, if not quite as picturesque a
sight in the Noviciate of the Fréres des
Ecoles.  It is certain they have been disturbed, drafted into the common barrack-
room to serve their military term, by the
votes of those "emancipators of the
race" — the Republican deputies of modern
France.  There were not enough soldiers,
without disturbing those devoted instructors
of the poor!  Will any one solve the
mystery — why so many men and women
are found to hate, storm, and rage against
everything that is really pure and good?
If any one doubts there is a devil, let him
ponder that fact.  Left and right of that
river Seine, there is heaped up as much
human defiance of God, and depravity, as
could well cumber any given, equal space
of this earth's surface.  Wedged in between — " *les extremes se touchant* " — you
have those *parterres* of virtue's finest
flower, to stay the suspended sword of the
Divine Avenger.

The Noviciates of the Great Society, S.
J. are everywhere.  There is one for each
of its twenty or so of *Provinces*.

But these three orders, by no means ex-
haust the list of those who seek their happiness and welfare in the common life, even
at the present day.  I selected them as

types.  They are not even as old, as some
others which still exist.  One has been
thirteen centuries in existence.  Millions of
men have passed through its ranks in that
time, and hundreds of thousands of women
through those of the female branch, dwell-
ing in perfect communism and purest
socialism.  This is the famous Order of the
Benedictines.  The Cistercians and Car-
thusians date from a thousand years back.
The Friars Minor, the Friars Preachers
and women's Orders of Carmelites, Fran-
ciscans and Poor Clares, six hundred or
seven hundred years.

Far from decreasing since the times of the
so-called Reformers of the sixteenth century, these associations of pious communism have had so prolific a growth that the
Council of the Vatican had it on its programme to devise a scheme for their
limitation, and the amalgamation at least of
those whose foundation was only of comparatively recent date.

And they all succeed!  It is surely worth
the while of our agnostic socialists to
inquire into the secret of that success.
If they are sincere, it ought to be of the
highest interest to them to know, that a
socialism and a communism in the best
meaning of those words, well regulated
and successfully conducted, do exist and

are actually practiced at this very hour,
and have existed so for centuries. This
they may see if they but use their eyes,
and may moreover learn the secret of this
amazing fact. For the men and women
who have gone apart, to tread the peaceful happy way of self-renouncement, have
enrolled themselves in no secret societies.
The conditions of their lives are perfectly
well known. Their friends and relatives,
from whom they are by no means severed
either in converse or affection, know perfectly how they live, why they so live and
are quite at ease as to their conduct and
welfare and — their sanity. There is a
certain class of people who do not weigh
this latter fact sufficiently, when they
officiously display their fears and anxiety
about conventual life. It should make
them feel, that they are meddling in a
business which is the immediate concern
of those friends and relatives to attend to,
and who do attend to it and are perfectly
satisfied, that it is all well with those who
are near and dear to them. This fact is,
also, a crushing refutation of the many
coarse and gratuitous assertions on this
subject, that rest as a blur and a blot on
many a page of English literature for the
last three hundred years.

Our agnostic theorists, and unsuccessful

experimentalists in the common life, will find that those other men and women have lived it, and died in it, because above and beyond this theatre of human passions, weaknesses and contentions, they lifted eyes of faith and held in view, as their goal, the life that ends not and knows no strife.

And they may rest assured, if they will only read the lesson of facts, that all other communism and socialism not founded in a faith like that, are simply impossible. There is no proof so convincing as experience. And if there is one experience more invariable in this world than another, it is that motives of faith have here succeeded, where bare human efforts have always failed.

In traveling the highways of the world, I have been surprised to find how many of our brethren, separated in the various sects, are strangely uninformed and misinformed about the great religious Orders actually existing in the Catholic Church. Whenever I attempted to describe them, they listened with either an air of incredulity or as if the tale were of some long-past romance. As for the many people who "believe nothing," I might as well have talked to them of the planetary beings of Mars or Neptune, so little did they suspect, that there were fellow-men around them leading such wondrous lives.

For such as these this chapter will not be amiss. "But surely you do not expect all the world to become Jesuits and nuns to improve their social condition?" By no means, but what I do assert is, that every experiment in socialism that is not founded, in a modified degree, of course, on the supernatural motives which inspire these great Orders, is sure to end in disruption and confusion. Without religion it could not endure.

---

## Chapter VI.

### Other Questions Not Answered by Science.

If the scientists, who ignore revelation, have presented us with only a very uninviting and somewhat slimy account of our origin, and are entirely mute before the question of what is to become of us, let us see, if they can satisfy or reconcile us to the state of things we have to endure in our intermediate passage between our cradle and our grave. The human life, transitory gift of each one of us, brief and sure to end, that is the problem of the highest interest to men.

Few there are who fail to feel how trying

and puzzling are its varying moods and
varied fortunes. "Moving accidents,"
there are, "by flood and field" — perils,
seeming injustices, fearful cruelties, unfair
inequalities, pain, sorrow, suffering, race
antagonisms, human slaughter by human
hands, until the earth is soaked in blood,
and human history grows red as we read.
Men want to know — Why should these
things be?

In another aspect, this planet of ours
looks like a huge penal settlement adrift
upon the sky. While all men are born to
work of some kind, nine-tenths of them are
condemned to hard labor for life. The lot
of the majority is a rough one, and their
condition is prolonged poverty, while
everywhere absolute pauperism is more or
less to be found. Suffering and sorrow
with impartial hand knock at every door.
There is no house, be it every so grand, or
ever so wretched, that has not, or has not
had, its secret sorrow and its chamber of
sickness, pain and death.

Why has it been so ordered and who has
ordered it so? Surely it was not man.

Each one's gift of life is a troublesome
thing. It demands constant thought and
care. Any relenting or neglect means
starvation, dirt, suffering and disease.
Each minute part of the bodily organization

must be administered to, and some of its functions are most humiliating. What is it in our nature, that makes some things painfully and shamefully repugnant to us, with no choice but submission to them? Life is threatened with fearful dangers. Think of the storms that rage, the hurricanes, tornadoes, the choking, blinding blizzards of winter, the sun-stroke of the summer-time, earthquakes, tidal waves (thirty-five thousand people destroyed in Japan the other day), of the annihilating lightning. When " the sea gives up its dead " that went down in doomed ships, what a host it will be ! When the graves of earth shall yawn, how many shriveled corpses will bear the scars of violent ends !

Think of the fierce beasts and poison-bearing reptiles, that lurk upon the earth where the sun shines hottest — the prowling tiger, that carries off between his powerful jaws living, agonizing Indian villagers to devour them at leisure in his lair, and the other " tiger of the sea " that bites through bones and flesh at a single snap — the deaf adder of the sugar plantations, whose swift sting paralyzes from head to foot with electric speed — the sword fish that pierces a body and lashes it to death upon the waves — the stinging sea slug that benumbs the swimmer, and strangest beast of all,

the man-eating man — the cannibal of
the Pacific seas !

Think of the wasting, desolating plagues
and epidemics, cholera, yellow fever, bubonic
malady, the leprosy. Men did not invent
such things surely — and while they are
laying their victims low in agony, no hand
from outside is interposed to check their
cruel course.

Perhaps the saddest feature of this world,
and fraught with ever-threatening danger,
are the inter-racial hatreds and aversions.
Three hundred millions of Chinese call us
" foreign devils" and " barbarians," and we
call them in equally complimentary contempt " chinkies " and " chows."   Two
hundred and odd millions of Mohomedans
curse us for " Christian dogs " and we call
them " unspeakable Turks," and though
their creed is " death to the Christians," of
which they often give startling illustrations
as recently in Armenia, yet when they ask
for loans of money we have witnessed the
strange parodox of Christians pouring millions of gold into their treasury — oh no,
not for charity or peace offerings but for
greed of the high interest offered, and the
wily Turk pats those fat bags of money
and says, " Ha, this will keep those Christian dogs from biting — they can not now
hurt our Moslem nation, for fear of losing

all this money — we have them safe in
'Turkish bonds!'" and so he slays Armen-
ian and Greek, and the bonded "powers"
stand around looking very foolish.

There are, besides, three or four hundred
millions of Brahmins and Buddhists as far
apart from us, and all the rest, as if they
came from a different Creator.

And when those race aversions reach an
acute stage, as they do from time to time,
and the races come into contact, the spirit
of human slaughter broods over men, and
the earth takes on the appearance of a pan-
demonium where the battles rage. At this
hour, what we know as Christendom, is one
vast military camp. Its component nations,
in dread and distrust of each other, are
armed with the deadliest weapons yet invented, and fleets of fearful engines of destruction ride the seas.

Some men, seized with a just alarm, are
agitating for peaceful arbitration as a substitute for war. But mankind and human
passions, being what they are, they agitate
for a Utopia. The godless recklessness
which is a product of the "scientific method," and which is so general in our times,
makes war inevitable, and its total abolition,
but a fond dream. Besides in such a state
of society as the present, war is not without
its uses.

But why should all this be?

And why — worse even than this — is it, that as soon as men begin to congregate in towns and cities, almost the first public structure they erect is a jail, to protect themselves from violent outbreaks of the vicious inclinations and the unruly behavior of their fellow-citizens? Jails are everywhere, and always well filled. Depravity and vice haunt the outskirts of every aggregate of humanity, and men have to tax themselves enormously for protection from their troubling and pervading presence.

Besides being a public danger, the ruin brought on individuals by moral evil, is in evidence on every side, and the petty, hateful passions that men bring into play against each other, embitter many a life, and mar the peace of social existence.

It would be pessimism to say that human life was made up only of this dismal catalogue of woes, and pessimism is false, and because it is false, it is also wrong. Much happiness is attainable and attained, and few indeed there are, who do not taste, at some time, the gladness of life. But *there* are those ugly facts which press us on every side, real and undeniable, and there is no reflective mind that does not impatiently ask — Why, why should these terrible things be?

And what answer have the agnostic scientists to give? Practically none — they *have* to notice them of course, but their explanations bear no message of comfort to men, they lead rather to despair.

The arch-agnostic Mr. Huxley confessed himself so puzzled by the woes of humanity, that he considered the happiest result would be, for some "friendly comet to collide with this wretched earth and end up the whole thing in destruction!"

Mr. Carlyle is represented by his biographer, Mr. Froude, as going about perpetually moaning and groaning over the "black confusion" of things on which, by the way, his thirty published volumes — the result of his much-lauded Golden Silence — shed not the smallest light for any one.

Mr. Herbert Spencer wraps himself in the clouds of the dark "Unknowable," and can not, of course, pretend to trace to any cause or permissive will, what is beyond the dispensation and control of men. The disciples of Mr. Darwin and the legion developers of his evolution theory tell us as a rule, that all these cruel facts proceed, in blind and powerless obedience, from certain fixed laws, whose end is to aid in the indefinite process of his great Evolution. All the facts of life are normal and natural, and under the exigency of law are working toward some final emancipation. Whether this explanation honestly satisfies themselves, is their own affair. It is but poor comfort to the actual and antecedent sufferers in this "Juggernaut" procession. There is no man who does not feel, that his is a personality distinct and separate from every one else — all his own. "What is to become of me?" has a most intimate and exclusive interest for each individual person, independently of every one else, and it is profoundly disappointing to be told, that this personality, of which I am so intimately conscious, is but an irresponsible factor in the vast process of evolution; an atom of a great aggregate borne upon an irresistible tide — whither — no one knows. Over and above this dismal spoliation of our personality, no information, as already stated, is given us, as to how we came to be cast into this whirling evolution, what good it is to do or what benefit is ultimately to be derived from it.

Thus the "scientific method" has left the world in a very unsatisfactory plight, and it is little wonder that confidence in its high promises of emancipating thought, liberating the human mind from superstitions, and elevating our intelligence, has weakened considerably.

But if the teachings of the "scientific

method" be cheerless and unsatisfying to the individual, the logical results of its influence on private conduct are disastrous to society. If men believed about themselves what they read in the agnostic science-books, and proceeded to act on what they learn from them, the world in the long run would become well-nigh uninheritable. The First Cause of our being, it is there stated, is not only unknown but unknowable and the final cause just as undiscoverable; it then becomes at once clear to men that they have no final responsibility for their conduct to any one. An unknown authority is no restraint on conduct, to a nebulous judge men give no sort of care, and we all know to what human conduct, without restraint, leads. The moment a man professes the principles of the "scientific method," which unfortunately is too often done in the foolish phrase, "Oh, I have no religion; I do not believe in anything!" you may quite fairly suspect that man in every relation of life. Suspect his honesty. With his principles, it would be quite foolish of him not to cheat, and turn everything else to his own advantage by fair means or foul — when it can be safely done. Suspect him of being hard-hearted, selfish and unfeeling. Why should he not be, if it suits him? He knows no authority over

his personal feelings. Suspect him of
being vindictive and revengeful. He will
pursue relentlessly whoever crosses or in-
jures him. To gain his revenge he will not
stick at secret murder. Why should he?
If he can be safe from men, there is nobody
else to fear.

Suspect his chastity. There are very
few, if any-at all, who are not intermit-
tently solicited by lustful fancies. Will
this agnostic, who spurns accountability
and writes down divine commands as super-
stitious lies, hesitate at indulgence wherever and however he can, when so inclined?
His logic would call him a fool if he did.
Thus the free-thinking disciple of the
"scientific method," unconsciously proclaims himself an object of distrust to his
fellow-man in every dealing and social
relation of life, and they in turn would be
very foolish not to distrust him. Mutual
trust and confidence are absolutely necessary
for decent and tolerable society. The
agnostic principle, if rigidly followed, utterly destroys those pleasant bonds, and
society ceases to be either tolerable or
decent.

Moreover, the basis of justice, on which
human laws rest, is undermined by the
scientific method in its account of human
existence. Why should a judge impose a

penal sentence on one who quotes the
agnostic evolutionist (whom a great part of
the world delights to honor) for his assertion, that he is under the spell of a natural
law impelling him to struggle for existence,
and that there is no being known to nature
who has given prohibitory commands, or
who will bring him to account? He can
plead from their text, that his impulses are
nature's work, not his. Why punish him
for them? It is unjust. He is but an irresponsible factor in the great evolutionary
process. When he cheated and stole, and
revenged and murdered, in the whole story of
human life as told him by the evolutionists,
there is not a shred of evidence to show
him guilty of moral wrong or wickedness.
There have been, and are in our days agnostic judges, Bramwells and Stephens, on
whom the accused could turn, and declare
from their own beliefs, or want of them,
that their laws have no foundation, and
their courts, frauds on poor evoluted humanity.

The same would apply to domestic rule
and parental authority. The children could
turn on agnostic parents and demand by
what right they corrected or punished them,
for the peccadillos and unruliness to which
all children are prone, but which make family life impossible if unrestrained. The

7

children can appeal to nature and impulse, sacred in the eyes of agnostic parents, and deny that they are in fault, and no fault, therefore no correction — why punish a poor evoluted mud-fish? how expect moral rectitude in a lepidosiren or conscience in protoplasm? The "scientific method" cries out against such things.

Thus carried to its logical conclusions in practical life, agnostic science would up-turn human society from its very founda-tion, and convert this earth into a pande-monium.

The clear perception of this has shaken the confidence of many minds in this much-praised " method" of dispensing with all information from the supernatural, and they are turning back again to the old ground for a more rational account of themselves, their lives and their destiny.

---

## CHAPTER VII.

### The Alternative of Science.

In contrast to the unaided and self-reliant "scientific method," let us recall what the old story, believed for so long a time, and by so many, to be revealed, tells us about ourselves.

It certainly has the merit of presenting a picture of our origin, which does not repel or put us to shame. Of recent years that picture has been kept a good deal out of the common view, " skyed " by the men of science. It has moreover been smeared over by much protoplastic mud, so that like a palimpsest manuscript, we must do some scraping to get at the original etching — which means that it is not easy to induce people, nowadays, to go over again carefully, so familiar a lesson as the Scripture story of the creation. But compared to the dismal tale of the scientists on the same subject, it is absolutely pleasant and most flattering to us. In place of mud swamps where " lepidosirens " swim and slumber, it introduces us to a fair garden where golden fruit is on the trees. Cool, clear streams are flowing on the carpet of green, through the glades, a wondrous variety of animals, tame and gentle, peacefully browse, and birds of every hue float and sing in the blue above.

There is one form just moulded and still lying upon the earth, but far finer and more perfect in line than any animal. And over that still inanimate form, the Great Maker, God, it is said — and said, remark, without any explanation or apology of wearying demonstration, just as a matter of course,

taken for granted as the great first logical
necessity that all right reason demands and
postulates — God breathes! That creative
and mysterious secret — the *spiraculum
vitae* — life from the Divine breathing,
courses at once through the finely mod-
eled members of that prostrate form — t
glows and moves, the eyes open and light
up the features with intelligence, and
then this last and greatest of the Creator's works rises and stands erect — the
first living man. That is what we infer
from the plain reading of Genesis, and what
men for ages have been satisfied with, and
proud to believe. But in these later times
it seems that this will not do at all. It is
too simple, too plain, too nursery-story-like
for the trained and powerful modern intellect. Facts, it is alleged, have been
brought to light by intelligent research
which prove that this was not — could not
be — the way in which we were made.
The human mind is surely very perverse in
this, as in other well-known things. You
would suppose, that a handsomely set-up
being like man, should be very glad just to
find himself so, without inquiring too
minutely how he came to be so gifted a
being — the first, the superior among all the
visible living things on this earth. But no,
that position does not suit our moderns.

They want to sweep away that privileged pre-eminence as a childish fable, notwithstanding the visible evidence all around us, and reduce man to the same common level of origin with the animals, no greater specifically, no better essentially. "Grant," says Mr. Darwin, " a simple archetypal creature like a mud-fish with five senses, and some vestige of a mind, and I believe natural selection will account for the production of every vertebrate animal." Well, well, I much prefer the other story.

And that story, so long held by so many of our race as a sacred tradition, continues with a still more interesting simplicity. Adam, our prototype and first father being thus fashioned, the Great Creator makes over to him and his, with a generous bounty that men forget, as a gift forever, all the other wondrous works of his creation. He made him lord of creation, with dominion over every living thing. In trial of his ownership, Adam summons all living things to his presence, and lo, they obey his call! Submissively they defile before him, and as they pass, he names them according to their kind. But, as yet, there is a certain loneliness in his state. These animals are fair to see in the grace and freshness of their primal type, but from not one of them all comes back,

to their new master, an answering
voice of intelligence — no communion
on equal terms of soul and mind. The
Great Maker, however, does not leave
him in that loneliness. He prepares a delightful surprise for him. He throws him
into a deep sleep, and as he slept, by some
mysterious process of creation, not at all
necessary for us to know, and which with our
present limited intelligence, it is impossible
for us to understand, he took from Adam's
substance, material out of which he builds
up another form like to his own, and sets
it over against him to look on when awak-
ened. With what delight and wonder,
must he not have gazed on this new thing
of exquisite beauty. He had seen the animals, and doubtless admired their wonderful formation, but what animal of them all
showed anything like to that in shapeliness
of form and comely grace? Its shape is
like his shape, but, oh, more finely, more del-
icately, more exquisitely moulded! It moves
and speaks, it comes toward him. Adam
peers into those eyes on a level with his
own, with joy he beholds a responsible
intelligence in their light, and in rapture
exclaims, "Now truly is this the flesh of
my flesh and the bone of my bone," and he
hails the first woman as "Eva — the mother of the living." This is how it reads in

the old, old story. No mention being made of an "archetypal creature like a mud-fish with five senses and a vestige of a mind," the scientists laugh it to scorn. "I would give absolutely nothing," says Mr. Darwin, "for natural selection, if it requires miraculous addition at any one stage of descent." "I hope," said Mr. Tyndall in his Belfast address, "to find in matter the origin of all terrestrial things."

To talk of the miraculous at the beginning of things, where all is miracle to us, seems shallow, if not impertinent. It is irritating to think that puny men, who pass away after a brief life, fancy themselves competent from a mere examination of fossil animal formations, to enter the domain of the Creator, and infallibly insist that the great mystery of life began in the way they think they have discovered, and in no other.

In view of the fact that the scientists in many countries, nowadays, regard the theory of evolution as a scientific truth, some of our writers, it is true, maintain that evolution is perfectly compatible with the story of Genesis, as far as the corporal formation of the race is concerned. Very well. If they wish to enter upon that experimental interpretation of the sacred Scriptures they are free to do so. The Church does not forbid it, provided they hold by the dogma that

God, as Creator, is back of it all. But let them not forget, in their enthusiasm for scientific research and their complacent acceptance, as scientific truths of the generalizations from biological and geological facts, that it is precisely that dogma which their agnostic friends want to have ignored. From their own avowal it is perfectly well known that their object is to dispense with the necessity or even the supposition of a Divine Creator. To our orthodox enthusiasts for evolution this should be a note of warning, not to allow themselves to be led too far afield. I know they say there is no danger; we can admit all the postulates of evolution and still assert that they are but the Creator's *modus operandi.* That they can do this is not at all so clear. If you admit a common protoplastic origin for *all* living things, and a subsequent transitional change from species to species, how differentiate between rational and non-rational creatures? how explain responsibility and non-responsibility, accountability and non-accountability? Where does the rational basis of *man's* nature come in? At what stage of his evolution was it added on? Was it as he was passing from the mud-fish into the reptile, or from the reptile to the bird, or from the bird to the quadruped, or from the four-footed to the four-handed

animal, or finally from the erect quadrumanous, "furnished with a tail," into the
man? Where, and when, and how, did
our rational nature accrue to us? Whence
the soul, with its moral sense and aspiration
for immortality? Evolution has not only no
word to tell us about that, but it is impossible to see how it can come into the theory
at all. The truth is, biologists and geologists can legitimately argue on the subject
of creation only *a posteriori*, that is from
the few facts they have been able to marshal
from the skeletons of animal life, the
process of generation, and the surface of
the earth. This, we all know, to be an
imperfect and fallible method of deducing
universal conclusions or establishing general
rules. When scientists pass to *a priori*
statements, that is, lay down how the
creation *must* have taken place, they are
guilty of the fallacy known to logicians as
the *transitus a genere ad genus* — a fraudulent skip from one position to another
position altogether different, and then pro-
claiming from the second what they purported
to have found in the first. To make *a priori*
infallible statements as to the manner of
creation (which they do with seemingly
great security), they must either be more
than men and share the creative faculty
themselves, or have stood on the level of

the Creator's platform while He was working, which is of course absurd. No matter what may be its merits as a theory, evolution proves far too little for us as rational, responsible and accountable men, and so will never satisfy us. It has no practical value for us as a light upon the *meaning* of our origin or ourselves, and may just as well be relegated to the glass cases of museums as a curiosity or conundrum of scientific speculation. The other story is more comprehensive and satisfying — it is certainly more agreeable, and it is as elevating as it is encouraging. It gives us an exalted idea of ourselves, to know that we are descended from a first pair, a man and woman fashioned by an Almighty Creator, and endowed with an intelligence far above the rest of His works. Secure in that thought, we are safe from the despair which must beset those, who believe that they have been cast out, unacknowledged and disowned, by some unknown and brute cause, into the whirling mass of the evolutionary struggle. We feel that there is an intelligent ownership back of us, and a Fatherhood above us, which will not permit the existence we have received, to be merely a torture and a mockery nor the aspirations implanted in our breasts — dreams of Tantalus.

There is hardly a doubt, that the many
who are turning away dissatisfied with the
conclusions of Agnostic Science, will find a
more secure and peaceful refuge for the
mind in the opening words of the ancient
creed — "I believe in God the Father,
Almighty Creator of heaven and earth and
of all things."

## CHAPTER VIII.

### "Lachrymæ Rerum."

If the story science has to tell us of our
origin be an uninviting one, still more dreadful are its lessons about the evils of life.
As an explanation of the harassing problems of existence, with its manifold evils,
and the "tears of things," the bare theory
of *natural selection, struggle for existence*,
and *survival of the fittest* is revolting. Applied to sentient and intelligent beings, it
implies the infliction of a shocking, mean-
ingless cruelty — a blind, wanton injustice
on the poor human race. For those who
feel overborne by the evils of life, evils that
are very real and very terrible, and have
nothing to stay them but this bald theory

of struggle and survival, what refuge log-
ically remains but

> "To take arms against a sea of troubles
> And by opposing end them,"

or to express it without poetry — commit
suicide! Many are doing so now, almost
daily, in countries where, formerly, that
stupid revolt against the Giver of life, used
to be extremely rare. Suicide clubs, we are
told, have even been formed. Modern suicide has thus assumed a cool deliberateness
where, before, it used to be the unreasoned
act of a wild despair.

This is quite as it should be, according to
the "scientific method" of accounting for
things. If there were nothing but that,
it is a proper and a wise thing for the unfortunate to kill themselves. But, happily,
the great majority of rational beings hold
the act of self-destruction, no matter how
heavily life's fardels weigh, as a thing to
be abhorred. Why? Because they evidently do not trust the "conclusions of
science," they look elsewhere for the
something more sustaining that "gives them
pause," before that dread and tragic act.

They find the motive in the old story of
revelation. Millions have found that sufficient motive before them, millions find it
now, and millions will continue to seek, and

find it sufficient, in spite of the fatal deductions from agnostic science.

The origin of evil has ever been the puzzle of the human mind. The ancients sought its solution in the absurdities and superstitions of polytheism. In the early Christian centuries an Eastern monk, in a clumsy, but perhaps pious effort to free God from any share in it, imagined his two eternal and coequal Principles, one essentially good, and the other essentially bad, so that every good thing comes from the one, and everything bad from the other. This blunt logic all metaphysicians agree to call an absurdity, since two eternal and opposing Principles are impossible. This doctrine had an immense vogue at the time, and Manicheism, as it was called from its author, counted numerous followers for nearly three centuries. Carried to its strict conclusions in practical life, the sect became a nuisance and a scandal, and its teachings and practices were many times refuted and condemned. It is strange that we should see in our day a revival of this exploded system with the same good-natured motive of finding a convenient escape from difficulties about the nature of God. Very recently a little book called "*Evolution and Evil*" was published in Edinburgh, in

The Creator was displeased. Could anything be more just or natural than that He
should have been? The first parents fell
out of His favor. From being perfect in
their kind, as the highest and best work of
the mundane creation, made in the image
and likeness of the creating Divinity, they
deteriorated. The will, that opposed the
Supreme Will, lost its strength, the intellect, that shared the Divine knowledge, lost
its privilege, the image of the Deity was
blurred in their souls, and they stood in the
case of rebels. And when they began to
beget children, they could only beget them
of that nature in which they themselves were ;
could impart to them no other kind of nature,
when begetting them, and so we all came to
stand in the case of rebels, under a ban.
This is the kernel of the story. It is an account, and the oldest account, of how the
misfortunes, undeniable and ever-present, of
our race came about. It is at least an intelligible account, it is reasonable and most
likely. It has been very long in possession,
and before it is cast aside as a myth, something better ought to be proposed in its
stead. Have the agnostic scientists given
us any juster reason, why humanity is in a
penal state, why wickedness abounds, and
calamities afflict, and why there is no such
thing as perfect and long-continued happiness

or contentment, to be found in all this earth
of ours? By no means. Their statements
are most disheartening in presence of these
hard realities, and conduce to despair, and
they may thank the utter helplessness of their
conclusions, for the reaction that is steadily
setting in against their magisterial utterances.

On the other hand the story of the old
tradition is most hopeful in its sequel. It
tells of a restoration and the "blissful
state" to be regained, as Milton words it.
Such a theory gives a new and more hopeful complexion to human life; it makes the
struggle worth enduring, because it gives
an intelligible and stimulating meaning.
The struggle is comparatively brief, and at
the end of it, is the possibility of full and
lasting compensation for every danger and
every pain endured. Yes, says the scientists, if it were only true — the admixture
of the marvelous, such as the talking
serpent, savors at once of the mythical.

But why should it not be true? Is it because you have found no trace of it in biology and geology, that therefore it did not
happen? That would be bad logic. Meanwhile certain facts of life are there, and
you have not been able to assign any adequate cause for them. It is therefore unfair
of you to interfere with those who fall back
on the tradition of the race about them,

The first intelligent progenitors of our
race were sure to transmit a minute and accurate account of all that happened at its
beginning to their intelligent posterity. It
would be contrary to the human mode of
acting if they did not. It is incredible, that
they never should have mentioned a word
on a subject so deeply important to all posterity, and it is most improbable that what
they imparted was not carefully repeated;
at least substantially. So important is
it, as affecting human life and conduct, that
when it came first to be written down, multitudes have always believed, as a thing reasonable and quite to be expected, that the
writer was guaranteed by the direct action
of the great Creator from substantial mistake, or, in other words, inspired. It is
reasonable to believe all this, especially as
it assigns a sufficient cause for many things
in human life and character, otherwise absolutely unintelligible to us. With regard to
the marvelous incidents of the story, who
can tell what is possible or impossible to a
Creator of such wondrous skill and power
which, if we are not blind, we must
acknowledge him to possess?

Every man, not intoxicated to asphyxia
with his own puny conceit, must honestly
admit that he has no *locus standi* in
objecting to the ways selected by an Agent

immeasurably superior to him, to bring
about his purposes no matter how peculiar
or even grotesque they may now seem to
us. The matter being beyond our power
and outside our province to interfere in, it
is wiser to accept the only reasonable explanation, within our reach, of the strange
state in which we find ourselves. It is
more than merely wise to do it, it becomes
imperative, when we see its practical bearing on our actual condition in life and on
our ultimate fate. Look around on humanity in general as we know it. Is it not
a grandeur in ruins, rather than a bran-new
structure erected on flimsy foundations and
progressing gradually to completion? When
you look upon a stately ruin you never say,
Here is something gradually growing to
perfection ; how fair it will be to look upon
when completed ! No, you judge from this
shapely arch, that bit of tracery or those
broken pillars that originally it had been a
fine building. In the same way when amid
the fierce passions, meannesses and deformities of human nature so abundantly illustra-
ted for us by history, and made real to us by
our contemporary wars, our jails and courts
of law, we are able to trace remnants of a
far nobler condition in general impulses, in
deeds of gentle virtue, of self-sacrifice and
heroism — in love for the beautiful, the pur-

suit of it in art, music, in poetry — in the
yearnings for the good and the true, we
say, How beautiful it must have been before the ruin came! So that our personal
experience of humanity corroborates the
tradition, that man began with the perfect
human nature which some calamity disturbed
and shattered. Even when some meanness
or frailty overtakes us individually, the first
thought that comes in sober mements is,
"Oh, for shame, we ought to have been
above that!" showing that there is a remnant of a higher, nobler nature yet within
us.

There is nothing in the shape of man that
does not exhibit the remnant of a nobler nature. The blacks of North Queensland
are supposed to be the very lowest types of
humanity. If I may be pardoned a personal reminiscence, I wish to relate here
how I found that remnant even among
them. They were small incidents, it is
true, but none the less they illustrate what
I say. I was one day visiting a camp of
blacks who lived on the warm sand-dunes
inside a mangrove swamp, on the north side
of Cooktown harbor. In front of one of
the miserable huts which are only used as
sleeping places, being long, narrow and
scarcely three feet high, a poor old woman
was seated on the ground industriously

knitting, with very primitive implements, a small open-work bag, such as children might use for school-books. The material was the native twine made from dried fiber and dyed in different colors. Anxious to get a memento of the rude skill of this very backward people, who seemed to me in their homes to have touched the lowest rung of the human ladder, I put a silver coin in her hand and made signs that I wanted the bag. She looked at it and shook her head, which I took to mean that she would not part with it. It was not so, however. One of the men came up and managed to explain that she did not wish to give it to me unfinished, but would finish it as soon as possible and send it over to-morrow. Considering that it was a good four miles across the water, I thought the chances of getting it very slight, still I left her in possession of the coin and passed on. As we were at breakfast on the trellised veranda of the house at which I was staying in the town at 7:30 the next morning, two of those coal-black natives timidly approached, holding up that bag! Honorable, was it not, in that poor creature?

Another day, strolling by the shore, I saw some Chinese *bêche-de-mer* fishers bargaining with a native black. Their net, it appears, had got fouled in the deep chan-

nel some distance from the shore. These
blacks are famous divers, and the Chinamen
were inducing him to go down to free their
net. He at length consented, and put off
with them in their boat. At that moment
his wife, carrying a small child, came run-
ning down. It was too late to stop him, so
she stood with riveted gaze looking at that
boat. Beauty is not a strong point in those
poor people, in fact it is not a point at all,
but it was beautiful to see the play of fine
qualities of soul and heart in that poor black
face. The job turned out somewhat troublesome, and the diver had to make three
different descents to the rocky bottom, remaining down what seemed to be quite a
long time, each dive. While he was under
water the young wife seemed beside herself.
I do not think I ever saw such genuine
feeling expressed in any face, white or
black — there was tenderness, protest, devoted love in it, and when he came safe to
shore, relief with a sort of sad, reproachful
delight. Beautiful remnant of the nobler
nature even in the dregs of humanity! I
can not help adding in illustration of the
abominable meanness of man that, a few
minutes later, I saw those Chinamen cheat
that poor black! They put him off with
two ounces of coarse tobacco and a hand-
ful of stale biscuit, for a task that gold

coin would not have induced themselves to
undertake. The poor fellow took that
squalid pay quite meekly and went away.
There be yellow men, thought I, in some
things, lower than Queensland Blacks.

Is it not more rational to believe that such
virtues have been left in a nature once all
virtuous, and that such vices come from its
deterioration, than to assert that both are
developed out of mud-fish?

Mere science leaves man without hope in
his miseries. It admits them as facts; it
even points them out, but gives no satis-
factory reason why they are there, and supplies no motive for the patient endurance of
them. Doleful, indeed, if not cruel, is its
attitude in presence of the universal fact of
death. When the quickly passing life of
each individual is over, and he must leave
behind all he loved, prized, and strove for,
science stands by in pitiable and helpless
silence.

Not so the theories of revealed tradition.
It has the story of a reconciliation between
a displeased Creator and ungratefully delin-
quent creatures. The nature passed on to
their progeny by the first pair, after their
disobedience, is to undergo a process of
restoration by the proffered intervention
of the Godhead, and, by the fulfillment
of new and not very difficult conditions,

the title-deeds, forfeited by the bankrupt
parents, to the "blissful state," are to be
given back to all the children of men.
Here at once a meaning is given to human
life, the touch-spring is supplied to human
action. The trial and the struggle endure,
it is true, for each individual of the race.
But the very possibility of reinstatement is
an end worth his efforts. The great sanc-
tions for upright conduct are kept ever
present to him — immense reward for success — penalty for willful failure. These,
with the higher feeling of loyalty to the
intentions of the benevolent Creator, supply motive power to the whole moral
world. They are the real and efficient
agency for civilizing humanity, and have
been admitted and are still admitted by the
majority of men, to be the best the world
has got up to the present moment. They
have inspired and still continue to inspire
all that is best in heroic self-devotion.
They sweeten social life, help to the patient,
if not cheerful endurance of pain and sorrow, and altogether have proved far
too practically useful to the human family,
to be contemned and renounced at the
summons of a science, which has but a
gospel of darkness and despair to offer in
their stead. That which has been the
mainstay of millions of the most civilized

people in the past, and has best reconciled them to life in its varying fortunes, it would be most unwise to discard until at least something as good has been found. It is certain that the results of scientific research supply no such substitute. A great multitude in our time have been led away by the ably-edited pretensions of the scientists, and have laid aside the guiding motives of life derived from faith, relinquishing all external observances of religion. Yet the restlessness of minds has by no means abated. It shows itself, in many ways at this hour, to be as great if not greater than ever. The recent closing of the grave over many of the men who made the greatest stir in the mental world for the past forty years, has given food for sobering reflection to many of their disciples and admirers who, weary of the emptiness of their master's conclusions, are longing again for the comfort of a confident and unfaltering faith.

They found its formula, regarding our origin, in the opening words of the old Creed already quoted. The second part of that Creed gives motive and meaning for the human life they are actually leading: —
"And I believe in Jesus Christ, His only Son Our Lord, who for us men and for our eternal safety, came out of the heavens,

and took flesh through the Holy Spirit from
Mary, the Virgin, and was made man. He
was also crucified for us, suffered, and was
buried. And the third day He arose from
the dead and ascended to the heavens;
thence He shall come to judge the living
and the dead."

This describes the restoration of the race
and the final issue that awaits it. He who
raised it up again, helped it and made salvation possible for its members, will also be
their Judge.

" Oh, but this is bringing us back to our
catechism again — it is faith and most of it
must be taken on trust!" Precisely, and
why should you be ashamed of it? Lift
yourself above your little self and think of
the distinguished men — men whose tran-
scendent ability is admitted on all hands —
who at the present day all around you,
openly believe and advocate all that. Mr.
Gladstone does so, and who will deny his
superiority of intellect? England's great
Prime Minister Lord Salisbury believes it
all. England's Lord Chancellor believes
it, so does conspicuously her Lord Chief
Justice, so do most of her able jurists. So
do her ablest diplomatists Lord Dufferin,
Sir Rutherford Alcock (lately deceased
after a most distinguished career), Sir
Philip Currie, Lord Brassey and the present

able Ambassador to the Court of Russia,
Sir N. O'Connor. President McKinley
believes it, so do his living predecessors in
that highest of all America's positions, Mr.
Harrison and Mr. Cleveland. These are
but some of the great names, and is your
judgment likely to be of more value than
the convictions of such men as these?
Why, before such an array of ability on
the side of belief, the cynical apostasy of a
John Morley (vide his "Voltaire"), the
ravings of Thomas Carlyle as exhibited by
his trusty showman, Mr. Froude, and the
poisoned shafts of Prof. Huxley — the Bob
Ingersoll of England — seem impertinences
of no weight whatever.

Yes, the goal of the return from this unsatisfying agnostic science is faith, belief in
the communications vouchsafed to us by
the Great Master, Owner, and Maker of us
and of all things.

---

## CHAPTER IX.

### "Statio Bene Fida."

No one, at all observant of the signs of
his times, can fail to see this movement
away from agnostic science and back to

belief. But is there a sure haven for the unrest of the returning? If unfaith and faith were just two camps, the question would be simple enough. Unfortunately the ungovernable tendencies of human thought, its refusal to be restricted, its opposition to restraint, no matter how reasonable that restriction and restraint may be demonstrated to be, have divided the followers of faith into many camps. This being a fact and a sad one, it is too well known to be denied, and too real and present with us to be ignored. This domestic quarrel has been the excuse for agnosticism, and is the strong point with the remaining adherents of that forlorn cause. In any sincere effort, then, to be of use as a guide to the unrestful soul, after its incautious excursion into the bewildering maze of agnostic science, this unpleasant fact must be faced and honestly weighed.

True, it has the disadvantage of making the writer appear in the light of a special pleader for his own views, and special pleading arouses suspicion and arms prejudice. "Oh, he is fighting for his own side of course — all he says is sure to be biased in favor of the section to which he belongs." And so, when there are contending interests, it is hard to get a hearing for the special plea.

I therefore wish to avoid all appearance of that as much as possible, and merely invite the reader to the inspection of facts as they exist about us. Facts are the most persuasive of arguments. They are not so dry as polemics.

I suppose then that the intelligent wanderer, in quest of the dropped threads of his old faith, would like to give in his adherence to a body of doctrine about which there is no uncertainty, fluctuation, or dispute among its particular followers, rather than to one about which there is much dispute, divergence, and dissent among those who variously profess it.

I suppose he would prefer to join a body that has a long and continuous history, to one that has a much shorter and somewhat broken history. I suppose he would feel more secure in associating with a body which is numerically greater, while agreeing among themselves as a unit, than all other dissidents from that body put together and disagreeing among themselves. Now such exactly are the characteristics of the two phases of Christian faith which, as mere facts, visibly and undeniably confront him in the world to-day.

Everybody knows who Leo XIII is. He is the two hundred and fifty-seventh, in direct succession, of the pontiffs who held

Church is entirely independent as to authority and standard of belief, from the Greek-Russian and the German - Lutheran. Within the English fold, too, the right of private judgment prevails, and has been a powerful dissolvent. As a result there are nearly two hundred distinct and independent religious sects in England and throughout the wide domain of her colonial empire, and also in English-speaking America the same strange spectacle, in proportionate extent, may be witnessed. Indeed the ultimate logical result of this free private judgment seems to be — as many religions as there are men. And is it not a curious thing, that men demand a freedom in religious matters not permitted them in matters of State, or in other relations of life? The State does not tolerate private judgment about its constitution and its laws, if carried into practice, as it is, so unrestrainedly, in religion.

However, as a matter of fact, this is the other phase of Christian faith presented to actual view by the most civilized of the nations to-day. That this is pretty accurately their condition nobody can deny, as it is a thing of common and public notoriety.

Now is it likely that our friend will lightly commit his spiritual hopes and future welfare to such a Babel confusion of religious guidance? Common prudence and sound sense would deter him from so little promising a course. Besides if he hears of the prayer of the Divine Founder of the whole system — "*that the world may know, O Father, that Thou hast sent me, let these be one as Thou art in me and I in Thee*" — it will be clear to him, that there *must* be something very wrong about all these people, for they are not *one*, but two hundred churches. It would therefore be something more than imprudent, it would be rash and dangerous, to follow after their way.

If he is to subscribe in full to Christianity, from which, supposedly, he originally started out in quest of something new, he has but one alternative. The fact of the marvelous unity combined with great numerical strength, of historical tradition, will forcibly appeal to his logical mind and incline him to become one of the two hundred and fifty millions who own Leo as visible chief.

However, it must be admitted that he will be confronted with another fact, for which the restlessness of certain minds in other disrupted branches of Christianity is accountable. There have been many in our day who, not venturing to go the whole daring length of total unbelief under

the lead of agnostic scientists on the one
hand, and not content, on the other, to
rest under the restraining soul-discipline of
Christianity, have bethought them of the
Buddhistic faith of the Far East, which
seemed to them to impose the minimum of
individual obligation and to be free from
harassing complications of doctrine. Hence
the recent introduction of what has been
named Theosophy among the more civilized peoples.

I doubt if this curious cult will arrest the
attention of any capable or reflective mind
for any long time. It has had, however, a
certain vogue, and its present standing
may be examined not unprofitably. It is
as hard to get any precise statement of this
new *osophy* or of the Buddhism it is supposed to represent, as the late Professor
Freeman said it was to fix Freemasonry as
a historical fact, or come at any reliable
evidence about it (*Italy*, page 34).

In a certain American university the dissatisfied Christians of a philosophy-class
not very long ago, with a view to adopting
Theosophy as a substitute for the faith of
their fathers, invited a Hindoo Bonze or
priest, named Dharmapala, to give them an
authentic and concise version of Buddhism.
To elicit more readily what they wanted
to know, they decided to proceed by

way of question and answer, so they
put up the Hindu on the platform
of their hall for interrogation, and ap-
pointed their professor as leading cross-
examiner. But it soon appeared that the
professor was like a man diving on a rub-
ber surface, he could not get under. After
several questions, answered in the high-
flowing and vague style of the Hindus, this
professor, who himself was evidently tired
of the version of Christianity as taught in
one of the two hundred sects in which he
was brought up, seemed to lose patience
and exclaimed with an air of profound disappointment : " But all this scarcely differs
from what Christianity exacts." Nirvana,
being the heart of the system, the professor next questioned him about this. What
was its nature? how was it to be attained?
and when attained what was it like? On
these points Dharmapala discoursed in
grandiose and soaring phrases, to which
the examiner frankly declared he could attach no practical meaning. He finally
asked the learned Bonze to give them a
short, intelligible description of what they
might expect in the state of Nirvana; he
replied that " no one having yet attained to
it, it would be impossible to do so ! " A
full account of this proceeding appeared
in the San Francisco papers in the early

summer of the year 1897. But we have
not since been informed whether a
temple to Buddha has been erected in this
very eclectic Californian university.

An effort was made to popularize Buddhism among the upper classes in England
under the pontifical patronage of Mr. Edwin
Arnold before he was made a knight (and
there was a time when the English Court
would not have admitted an *English* Buddhist among its equerries), but it took no
hold there. The event of Madam Blavatsky
and Prof. Max Muller's able exposure of
that lady's ignorance and charlatan pretensions, may be considered the requiem of
Theosophy as far as England is concerned.
The theosophical priestess subsequently removed her headquarters to Paris. Among
a certain class of the French, ever ready to
experiment with the newest sensation, she
met with some success, but her poor, clumsy
conjuring with familiar spirits from the
Pamirs, was exposed by a fellow-country-
man, the editor of a St. Petersburg journal.
He wrote a biography of this Mrs. Blavatsky, and not the least useful of the labors
of the London Psychical Research Society
was the translation of that remarkable and
sadly interesting book and its circulation
over the English speaking world. How
any sane person could continue to pursue

this phantom of a faith after reading this book passes comprehension.

It is true that Mrs. Blavatsky's very erratic disciple, Mrs. Besant, published another biography enthusiastically favorable to her, but it was manifestly compiled from material supplied by the most interested of witnesses, the lady whose praises are sung.

It is also true that much has been said in favor of the purer forms of Buddhism, notably by Mr. Max Muller, and the word of that wonderful scholar is of great weight. But by the purer forms the professor is careful to explain, the high moral maxims which he found in its ancient writing. Surely we need not go to Ceylon or Thibet for high moral maxims! Are they not to be found as high as any one need desire in the book from which, with scarcely any doubt, Guatama Buddha himself and his disciples largely borrowed — the Old Testament — and which the New Christian Testament indorses and adopts?

Much is made, too, of the statement that Buddhism is the religion of three hundred millions of the human race. But far too much is made of this. Without due examination, that broad statement is certainly calculated to impress and disturb the ordinary un-Buddhistic mind. But, first, supposing them three hundred million — it may be asked, What is the quality of that portion of the human race? 'Are the people composing it among the foremost, best educated and most civilized peoples of the world? Surely not.

Again the statement itself is contested. Travelers, who have come from the Eastern lands, assert that this number, as representing those who are really Buddhists, is enormously exaggerated. I have seen it reduced by some writers to as much as one-tenth!

But even allowing for a very great number, it is beyond doubt that the divisions and differences among them in creed and practice far exceed even the fragments into which the so-called reformed-Christianity is split.

Almost the first object, that greeted the visitor to the last great World Exhibition in Paris, was a huge statue of Buddha. Any civilized man gazing at that most in-artistic, clumsy and stupid-looking travesty of the human form, must have felt nothing but aversion, and passed on, with a sigh of pity for the aberrations of the human mind, when abandoned to its own purblind groping for the great secret.

Mahomedanism will also greet our friend as another of the world's great facts in supernaturalism. To find what is attractive

or of value in that, he has but to do two
things — examine what historians who write
of the sixth century have to say of its
founder — that remarkable Bedouin camel-
driver of this period, and of his preceptor, the
ex-Nestorian monk. Next, reflect on what
is the lowest animal instinct in men and
what Mahomedanism promises and permits
in satisfaction of it. When he has done
this, it can be safely left to himself to say,
whether respect for his own intelligence
and regard for our weaker and gentler sisters, will permit him to enrol himself among
the followers of the prophet's present representative, whom an English statesman
has proclaimed to our age as " the great
Assassin."

He will encounter still another fact in the
world of religions, far less in proportion
than the last, but far greater in significance
and even mystery. He will see a people
some seven millions in number, scattered
through the world, owning no country, yet
as distinct and apart from all other peoples,
as if their " place and nation " had not been
taken away. If he read history aright he
will think gently of the Jew. He will forget Shakespeare's Jew — the worldly and
commercial Jew, that deals in " usance "
and " pounds of Christian flesh." He will
remember this people for their grand tradi-

tion. He will remember them as the progenitors of our whole race, as the chosen people of God, and of old time, His most favored nation. He will think of them as the people whose influence on the world stands first and without any rival; and he will think of them in the later time when, alas! they let their day go by, and standing belated by the wayside, allowed their sacred inheritance to pass to the Gentile. He will think of them then, as the poor outlawed, hunted race, driven and persecuted for weary centuries at the hands of those whom the divine compassion of their gentle Master, Himself of Jewish blood, should have taught humaner methods. He will recognize in their marvelous preservation a divine intention and a lingering of divine regard. He will recognize remnants of their greatness in their great intelligence which, when the opening comes to them, makes them still leaders among men, as it has at this hour made them princes in the world's commerce. And finally, he will remember them as the people of a prophecy yet to be fulfilled, which tells that their latest progeny on earth will be rallied to the spiritual kingdom of Him, whom their fathers, foiled in their mistaken hopes for national glory, rejected and delivered over to torture and to death.

It is not good in us to think unkindly of
Jews when the Master's latest prayer was
for their forgiveness.

They are a living fact in our world to-
day. In their creed they profess and possess the truth — the genuine truth — that
we too hold in honor — only they have
halted short of its divine fulness.

Such is the full prospect before those
who are returning disappointed and empty
from their agnostic experiences. If to the
careful use of their intelligence, they but
add a humble prayer for guidance and for
strength, there is little doubt which anchor-
ing ground will appear to them the *statio
bene fida* — the right trusty harbor for
their souls.

---

## CHAPTER X.

### Important and Practical.

The returning agnostic will find that in
the "safe harbor," indicated in the last
chapter, his love of science need not, by
any means, be shed at its entrance nor its
fascinating pursuit be necessarily abandoned.

Though the parent church of Christianity
does not assign the place of first importance

to the study of the natural sciences, she is
far from forbidding that study to her members. This very year 1897 gives a striking
proof of this. The Fourth Catholic Scientific Congress was held at Fribourg in
Switzerland at the end of the summer. The
most eminent Catholic scientists — and
their number is not small — were invited to
attend. The meeting was thoroughly
representative of the Catholic world.
There were delegates from Great Britain,
Ireland, the United States, France, Spain,
Italy, Austria, Germany and Belgium.
Two hundred papers, on scientific subjects,
were read at the sessions of the Congress.

Almost every branch of human knowledge was discussed — the social question,
law, history, political economy, physics,
mathematics, astronomy, biology, art, phi-
losophy, religion. Surely a syllabus ample
enough to satisfy the most ambitiously scientific. All these had their share of friendly
debate. The leading and most useful feature of the discussions seems to be an honest effort to determine what has been really
demonstrated in science and what has not,
thereby separating true science from that
which has not, as yet, established its title
to that august name.

The Head of the Catholic Church, far
from frowning on this enterprise, as fraught

with danger to matters of defined faith, sanctioned it by his permission and full approval.

But there is, besides, permanent testimony to the freedom of scientific pursuits within her fold, in the programmes of her higher educational establishments in all parts of the world. These programmes may be had for the asking anywhere, and a perusal of them will show how false it is to say, as Mr. Huxley unfairly said, that this church is always opposed to the study of science.

The pursuit of science in itself she has never opposed. But she has combated, and must always combat the *conclusions of certain scientists*, in which the existence of God is denied, or in which He is declared to be unknown and absolutely unknowable, and therefore is not to be counted or thought of at all in human affairs; in which the human soul and man's immortality are also counted out, and in which all revelation or knowledge, derived from Him who created us, about ourselves and the meaning of our lives, is to be rejected as a fraudulent and absurd invention — an imposture! Yes, these assertions alleged to be directly derived from science, the Church, and I fancy the saner and better part of mankind, will always contest and refute, maintaining that

they are not legitimate conclusions from
true and demonstrated science. Why they
are persistently asserted by men of name
before the world, is a secret of their own
personal and private lives which the great
accounting day will manifest. It is certain
the "conclusions of Science" favor the
freest kind of living. They act as mutes
on the strings of conscience.

The returning agnostic will find, too, in
the teaching and practice of that church,
not mere dry speculative dogmatism having
reference only to the life hereafter, but
much that is valuable in its practical bearing on the actual life of the world, much
that is of great service to society, curative
of its ills and fenders to its dangers.

What are the things which agitate and
alarm society at the present day?

1. There is the unrest of the masses of
the laboring poor — their awakening to the
consciousness of the fact that they *are* poor
and ill-provided with the comforts of life,
and are slave-driven in work which at best
is precarious, and from the profits of which
only the very slenderest share comes to
them, while there are a favored few into
whose hands enormous wealth has been
gathered, who have apparently bought
themselves free from general sentence of
toil, who live in extreme comfort and luxury,

and who command an abounding market of needy men to do everything for them, even to the increasing of their already great stores of riches. This glaring inequality is the root of the socialism, so universally discussed in our times, and is assuming such threatening attitudes against establishing order and peace almost everywhere now.

He will find in this church some very practical teachings to assuage this acute feeling, and mitigate the danger of its violent outbreak — if listened to.

In a former chapter I briefly, but truthfully, described numerous societies of men and women, who actually exist around us and have existed for a very long time, where comradeship and harmony prevail with perfect equality and unity of purpose for a common good — a good by no means restricted to self, but helpful to others, and a life, not ease-loving and indolent, but ceaselessly and devotedly active in the cause of ignorant, needy and suffering humanity. It is the supernatural motive — the reflex from the eternal life, and all they are taught about the will, the justice and the holiness of the Omnipotent, which alone makes the self-devotion, the self-immolation of such an existence, possible in this world. And it is the same motive and none other, ap-

plied of course in a lessened degree and
modified to meet the circumstances of
worldly occupations, that will restrain the
poor within the bounds of moderation
in their just efforts to better their condition, and guide them securely in the way
of happiness. It is through men's minds
the world is best governed — better than by
the ruder means of force and terror, and
unless it is ingrained in men how unwise it
is to give all their thought absorbingly to a
life so passing and so short, and practice no
virtue, which is the price of better things
in the more enduring one — in other words,
admit the supernatural into their thoughts
and daily lives — in vain will you propose
"nationalization of all the instruments of
production," "unification of labor," and
"equal distribution of profits," "land
tax" or "single tax," Fourier's "Pha-
lansteries," Comte's "Polity," or any of
those well-intentioned schemes for social
improvement, of which the last forty years
have been so prolific. Nor is the supernatural motive a nostrum, with which to
beguile the poor. It is for rich and poor
alike. The supernatural must be read-
mitted into the lives of both in much larger
measure than it is at present, before there
is the slightest chance of restoring peace
between capital and labor. It is quite cer-

tain that these benevolent schemes of the
Georges, the Marks, and the Morrises will
never succeed. With men, as they are
now, they are unworkable. That the
supernatural no longer occupies the prominent place it ought in the lives of multitudes of men in our time, is due mainly to
the wrangling and divisions of sects since
the sixteenth century. So the first step in
efforts to restore it would be, to bring
about a reunion of Christendom under one
form of faith.

But this, it will be answered, is as
Utopian as the schemes of single taxers
and nationalizers " of land and instruments
of production." I do not entirely admit
that, but I say that unless some approach
to it is made, notwithstanding the impious
sneers of a reckless minority, you may
despair of a settlement of the social question. Agitation and storm and fights will
come — violence and bloodshed will be witnessed again, but when their short season
is over, things will fall back into the same
if not a worse, state again — the future but
repeating the past. Mr. Benjamin Kidd in
his " *Social Evolution* " says that the
" altruism," on which the socialists depend
to make their proposals a success, is not to
be found in human nature. He maintains
that " the altruism, that ever did anything

or ever will do anything among men, has been generated by religion and religion alone.''

The late Professor Blaikie, whose sympathies were strongly in favor of a moderate socialist programme, also confesses in one of his essays that "the true altruistic spirit, necessary for the success of socialism, must come from the fountain of religion, and socialism must enter into closer alliance with religion." It is a pity that many will have to ask—"Which?" Socialism is as broad as humanity, and religion ought to be able to confront it as one, and with no faltering and uncertain doctrine. This latter condition, at any rate, our returning friend will find well fulfilled in the great church still united under Leo XIII, who, by the way, is acknowledged in our day as the best exponent of socialism in its highest and truest sense.

2. Our age is suffering, and in some places alarmingly so, from a deplorable change in women's view of maternity.

In France premiums have been offered by government for larger families!

Not long since a prominent New York physician, in an article contributed to the *North American Review*, raised the alarm for America on this delicate but most important subject. He declares it has become

the rule with American wives, either not to
bear children at all, or to have but one or
two at most. Among the causes to which
he attributes this dreadful state of things,
he notes "the loosening of religion's hold
on American parents." They no longer
regard its strict prohibition of this practice,
and have taken the matter into their own
hands. In the Catholic Church a most
succesful remedy is applied to this. The
practice and obligation there enjoined of
the regular "confession of sins," which has
come in for such aspersion at the hands of
the separatist Christians, but which is
really one of the greatest forces for moral
good in the world, though the least ob-
trusive and most silent, renders such deplorable practices impossible. Every Catholic
woman knows, that the benefit of this
sacrament would be uncompromisingly
denied, until all such sinful tampering with
nature's laws was completely abandoned.
And their faith in their church's teaching
always prevails.

It is not out of place to add here that the
prejudiced attacks on "the confessional"—
happily growing less in this more reasonable age—have no foundation in fact.
Here is a simple way to test it. You may
meet everywhere whole families, whose
members of both sexes have made it a

lifelong practice "to go to confession."
Ask any of them collectively or individually, if any harm or evil has come to them
from that practice? Their answer will be,
"No." Ask them if they ever heard
anything in that confessional that was not
for their good? You may rely on it —
their answer will be, " Never." The thing
stands to reason. If there were in this
practice adopted by millions of people, as
a part of their lives and so for many
hundreds of years, anything radically or
grossly wrong, it would have become
of such public notoriety long ago, that
no one of respectability would be found to
follow such a practice; but as many
follow it as ever — many most excellent
people, you will find, if you only take
the trouble to inquire, which proves that
a most unjust prejudice has been propa-
gated against it.

3. Our age is suffering from a loss of
respect for the sacredness of the marriage
bond. Facility of divorce, which now
nearly everywhere prevails under the un-
righteous usurpation of the civil power in
the domain of an institution directly
established and safeguarded by God Himself, has resulted in sad consequences to
society. It is not unusual for a woman
to meet at social gatherings two, three

and even four men to whom she had been
severally married! The disruption of
families follows — so many foundations of
civilized society uprooted. Children are
robbed of their homes, and neglected.
The filial feeling, hitherto so wholesome
and sweet an influence in life, is blighted
and ruined by a precocious knowledge of
the disgraceful frailties of parents.

The most repulsive feature in this authorized license of manners, is that the divorce
courts offer a premium and an invitation
to vice, for almost immediately the "re-
spondent and co-respondent" get married.
These shameless people often unblushingly
own that their infidelities have been com-
mitted so that the divorce court may have
evidence to set them free to indulge their
unnatural and illicit amours. And the
court obediently enters into their plot.

Against this manifest drifting into pagan
barbarism, the ancient Church stands firm.
It proclaims to the world, that marriage is
not a thing to be tampered with by any human authority whatsoever. "Whom God
has joined together let no man put asun-
der," is her charter on this. The yoke
which has been deliberately and validly assumed — it is God's will, she declares —
must be borne to the end. The marriage
bond is sacred — made by God Himself,

and given into the keeping only of those who represent Him. No marriages, she says, done in slipshod fashion over the counter of registry offices shall be blessed by her. No halting, conditioned form of marriage on which rests the gloomy shadow of a prospective divorce, and takes away from the young people that security of " settling in life " they so eagerly looked forward to, is permitted by her — it must be " for better, for worse till death do us part." And if in a minority of cases the yoke hopelessly chafes, and the couple prove ill-suited to each other, she meets that with the legal separation from " bed and board," but insists, that *for the common good*, the inconvenience of celibacy must be borne until the death of one shall set the other free.

4. Our age suffers from a lack of honesty in public and private life. People are beginning to be puzzled to know, what to do with their money, which prudent thrift rightly dictates to them to put by for " the rainy day." The exposure of gigantic swindles like that of J. Balfour, ex-M. P., &c., the wholesale plunder of the Panama stockholders, the "booming" of worthless or fictitious properties and stocks as investments, awaken the world, from time to time, to the fact that multitudes of men

have lost all conscience about stealing the
money of others. The expensive excite-
ment of "turf" and "ring" gambling
has created a passion for petty pilfering
which leaves no employer safe. The system of electing office holders and judges
only for a short period, has opened the
door to corruption and dishonest jobbery
of all kinds, where that system prevails,
until people get little value for their taxes
and can scarcely get justice fairly administered.

To this serious and dangerous wrongdo-
ing, the Church firmly opposes the "refusal of absolution in confession" to the
thief and cheat, no matter of what rank or
position, until restitution be made to those
who were wronged, and until robbery in
every form be abandoned. The world little
knows the powerful help it lost in its
affairs, when the separating Christians
of the sixteenth century decreed to dis-
continue the practice of confessing their
sins.

5. Our age is suffering from a loss of
what may be called, for want of a less awk-
ward word, *femininity* in women. An am-
bitious spirit has entered into them. They
are hungering for a share in all public
affairs, and aim at abolishing all distinctions of sex in the avocations of life. Why

may not we do everything that men do? they say. And they proceed to do it — never reckoning how much of their charm they shed with their skirts. They stop not even at skimming the highways and dashing through our streets, in that new and least modest of postures — astride of a bicycle.

Well, the Church has nothing *de fide* on the manners of women, but she has plenty to restrain their excesses in the wise traditions from which she does not intend to depart, and in the golden rules for women's conduct which she has by no means abrogated. She has quiet, but sufficient, means to see to it that her children, who are styled in her liturgy the *devotus femineus sexus*, shall not make themselves — instead of helpful examples in modest reserve — wanton occasions of spiritual hurt to men. Women owe their present high place in civilization, as well as their rescue from a barbarous degradation in past times, exclusively to the action of this ancient Church. They should, not ungratefully, remember that. If they choose to forget it, and despise her counsels, so wise from long experience, it is certain they will fall back into the same cruel subjection again. Let them turn their eyes to the Orient! Who of them would be Moslem women or Hindoos? Well, to that, the half-unsexed woman of to-day is inevitably hastening her sisters of the future!

Thus our friend will find that the practices and teachings of this oldest Christian church, are by no means all dry mysticism or valueless speculation. All the other way. There is hardly a detail of human life on which they have not a direct and beneficent bearing, and undoubtedly make for the true civilization and happiness of the race.

A signal service was rendered to the Christian world when the Council of Trent, amid the mental confusion of the sixteenth century, issued a clear and unhesitating re-statement of the whole Catholic creed. The straying agnostic would do well to refer to that settled standard of faith for further details. Many editions of it have been published in the Latin tongue as well as in translations, and may be procured from any Catholic publishing house. True, since that time two points of doctrine have been defined — the Immaculate Conception of the Blessed Virgin Mary and the Infallibility of the Pope *quoad fidem et mores*. But *defining* does not mean inventing. It does not mean that those points were not hitherto believed. On the contrary, it is an affirmation that they *were always accepted* as true by the Church generally, but that no pressing need of formulating them as beyond all dispute, that is, *defining* them, having arisen, they were not, hitherto, incorporated in set terms, among the articles of faith.

CHAPTER XI.

### Present Day Dangers to Believers.

There never was a time when " the just man living by faith " was more exposed to disturbing influences than he is at present.

1. Magazines and Reviews have multiplied to an enormous extent. They are not what they used to be. They have no particular views, no principles, take no sides, and represent no party. They open their pages impartially to error and to truth alike. They are open debating ground, from which no subject is excluded, where nothing is sacred any longer, nothing exempt from the most searching and adventurous criticism. Side by side with an interesting account of travel or some question of politics, you have a fierce onslaught on the Bible, on some particular point of be-

lief or religious practice. To take a haphazard instance look at the *North American Review* for December, 1895, where Prof. Goodwin Smith disports his Voltaireanism. Look at almost any number of the London *Nineteenth Century*, or of the *Fortnightly Review*, the same medley of confusing views on every aspect of religion and the supernatural may be encountered. This species of literature has a very wide circulation and makes favorite short reading for hosts of men who are too busy to study things *au fond* or read whole books. There is little doubt that this literature is accountable for much of the unbelief and of the unsettled belief, that prevails.

It is, then, a danger to the believer.

But what is to be done about it?

It is hopeless to expect, that the unrestrained liberty of the press in this particular will be interfered with. No government cares any longer to intervene in favor of religious belief. *As* governments they ignore the fact, that God has rights over the minds of his creatures.

It only remains then for individuals, who do care for faith, to refuse to aid and abet such publications until their editors and publishers show more solicitude to safeguard religious belief.

" Oh, what narrow-minded advice ! People ought to know all sides of questions ; it
is unfair and cowardly not to listen to what
every one has to say." To this remon-
strance, which will at once be made in
many quarters, the Catholic believer at least,
can most reasonably answer, that he does
not choose to employ himself so idly as
reading denials and contradictions of matters that, for him, were settled ages ago by
expert authority, which he deeply respects,
and on which he has long since made up his
mind, that it is safer and wiser for him to
rely. It is not cowardly — it is common
sense and prudence not to listen to people,
who only succeed in upsetting the mind on
subjects which he deems very vital to his
happiness, and who have nothing at all to
offer in place of the hope they deprive
him of, and leave him only in bewilderment.
It is not unfair in him to demand, at least, the
liberty of not listening to very bad and very
unpractical advice. Take for instance
Goodwin Smith's article above referred to.
He seeks to undermine all respect for the
Bible, and flatly denies it to represent God's
instructions or the expression of His will to
His creatures. Well, what are we to
accept in place of it? Mr. Smith's
instructions to the world? Hardly !
For hundreds of years this question

was deliberated upon, again and again, by intelligent, educated men, men of cultivated intellect, of different nationalities and different times, and they all have delivered a unanimous verdict in favor of this most ancient and venerated of books. That ought to be enough for any ordinary man, and the believing Catholic knows that it is enough for him. Nor does he feel he is surrendering his reason or his judgment in any way. He rather feels that he is vindicating his common sense and acting as all sensible men do in the ordinary affairs of life. There are legislative bodies and Supreme Courts of law everywhere. No reasonable citizen ever thinks he is surrendering his reason or judgment in accepting their decisions, and on occasion he is willing even to surrender his own private judgment, as the wisest and safest thing for him to do. If any one button-holes him and lays out arguments to prove to him that he should not do so, he says: "That is foolish talk," and he does not listen. Every sensible man applauds him for that. On subjects that to him are of much higher importance than State laws, why refuse to the believer the same approval that the citizen is sure to get for acting so sensibly?

Or take Mr. Huxley's assertive articles in the *Nineteenth Century.* Why should

the believer waste time in reading what
hundreds of men, whom he knows better
and respects more than Mr. Huxley, have
told the world long ago were matters fixed
and decided on as of faith, and founded on
divine authority? All the Huxleys in the
world could not change his opinion now,
and even if they could they have nothing
to offer on which he could rest for courage
and hope as he rests on his present belief.

Therefore the best and only thing to do
is to leave those men and dangerous literary
symposiums severely alone. When you are
walking out peacefully with a sound head
and whole skin, and rocks are flying about,
you do not go deliberately in the way of
them. "But," it will be answered again,
"Cardinals Manning and Newman and Gib-
bons contrbuted to the pages of these
magazines."

That these distinguished men felt impelled
to reply to outrageous attacks on revelation
wherever opportunity afforded, is by no
means a formal approval of the methods
adopted by the publishers of those new eclectic periodicals. Probably they were glad
of the chance to turn an evil, they could
not abolish, into a vehicle for at least some
good. Moreover there is no need to have
recourse to these monthly papers to find
out what these eminent churchmen have

to say; that may be found, in better and
fuller form, in their own published works.
 2. *Free Public Libraries* are another
danger. They are everywhere the rage in
our days. Though free they are in another
sense compulsory. People are compelled
to pay for them in taxes, if private munifi-
cence has not stepped in to build and endow
them. In another sense too they are really
free — very free indeed. There is no censorship for any kind of book, except the
openly obscene. The shelves of those
libraries are as impartially open to irreligious falsehood, attacks on faith and the
supernatural, and to religious truth, as the
pages of the new symposium journals.

These library buildings, all handsome,
substantial structures on which public
money is unstintedly lavished, are said to
have many advantages. They are nice cozy
shelters for the poor and unemployed. No
one will grudge them for that purpose,
though no doubt something less pretentious
would do in most places.

They keep the working classes out of sa-
loons and gambling places. This is a
matter of statistics that I am not competent
to deal with, but if they do — and do them
no worse harm, supply no poison for their
souls — all right.

They are a great help to the poor scholar

and intelligent mechanic where books beyond their slender purses may be consulted—
excellent.  The best and newest literature,
history, travels, fiction, etc., is there within
easy reach of all who cannot have home
libraries and who, out of working hours,
are fond of reading and self-improvement —
admirable too, only it must here be added
that from universal experience the heaviest
demand is always on the fiction department,
especially by the youthful of both sexes, so
the " self-improvement " is of a shady and
doubtful kind.

They add to the culture and refinement,
lessen ignorance and keep up education
among the people.  The experiment is too
new, to pronounce yet with confidence, on
these happy effects.  It should be the wish
of every one that they may do so.  But it is
just possible that just such miscellaneous
reading may have a lowering effect on
morality.  And what will compensate a
nation for that calamity?

Further than that, and a greater calamity
is it to leave a people without any religious
faith whatever.  This is the recorded conviction of the wisest men in every generation.  And beyond all doubt these free
Public Libraries in one respect contribute
to this danger.  In nearly every one of
them, on demand, you can obtain any of

the books that contain the most virulent attacks upon religious belief for the last hundred years.

And what is to be done?

We can not send Samsons through the world to pull them down. We do not boycott them like the symposium magazines — we should be summoned for taxes all the same.

There remains only reform. Every rate-payer, with a conscience for his country, should agitate for a stricter censorship over all books of a dangerous tendency, and the appointment of competent and upright censors. As no discrimination is to be hoped for in favor of any particular theological works, owing to the unhappy confusion introduced by the sects, *eliminate that department altogether* from the public libraries — allow no books of any kind treating of religion. That is about the best that can be done, and any body of united rate-payers could easily insist on it.

3. Legislators declare that this had to be done in the *Public School* system. The multitude of contending sects, they said, left them no choice, but to drop religion altogether from public education. This may be a good argument to make use of for purifying the Public Libraries, where the omission can do no harm.

But unfortunately such action, as applied to daily training of young children, constitutes the greatest of all dangers to the religious faith of a country, and, as experience is every day abundantly proving, is accountable for the vast amount of religious indifference among the adult population, wherever that system prevails.

It is a fallacy to say, that dropping all religion out of education was the only choice left to settle the question. There is more than one way of settling it.

If the body of men in charge of state affairs deem it, in their might, incumbent upon them to prescribe what kind of education the people's children shall receive — a right which is by no means incontestable — then, rather than close the school-room door upon all religion, they should have first tried, if they themselves still retain any due reverence for God's rights, less · sweeping and less perilous measures.

The people are divided into two classes. One maintains that religion forms a part, and the most important part, of education. The other says it does not. Meanwhile the State, assuming the duty of educating the nation, levies taxes for the purpose from all, and yet positively refuses to have anything to say to religion. In the eyes of the first class, and they are no inconsiderable num-

ber, as the State fails in an essential part of
its duty, they question the justice of the tax.
But as they can not resist the might of the
State, they obey the law under protest, and
peacefully suggest another way out of the
difficulty. They say, Remit us our proportion of this public tax, which we promise
to apply to the education, that includes
religious training for our children. That
seems perfectly fair and just.

Legislators reply that this would be cum-
brous and troublesome. Yes, but if it is
fair and just and right, is it not worth the
trouble? Does it not make the trouble a
duty to that class of citizens?

They also make answer, that it would
breed divisions in the country to the danger
of the State. The advocates of religious
training meet this with denial. They protest their loyalty to the Constitution, and
offer any guarantee the State may see fit to
exact, in the way of inspection of their
schools and vigilance over their methods, in
proof of their good faith.

It is objected, in the third place, that it
would break up uniformity in the standard
of national education, which everybody
admits ought to be maintained.

Well, so do the religious educators admit
it, and profess themselves ready to adopt
the State standard in all secular branches,

where they do not clash with their religious views, which is only likely to happen in the subject of history — and they are moreover willing that the efficiency of their schools should be tested by State educational experts.

Could any demand be more manifestly fair than theirs, surrounded by such safeguards?

Why is it not granted then?

Because there is another large class, who want to fling over all religion, and who know that the present system admirably helps their desires. This is a proof of the danger to all belief, which results from these schools.

And (2) there is another equally large class whom, unhappily, sectarian jealousy, and long-cherished animosity to another section of their fellow-citizens, place in opposition to everything desired by them — "We will not listen to any demand *you* make or any plea *you* put forth," they say; "we suspect and distrust you." Shame! And this is a country which boasts of perfect freedom and toleration! In face of such opposition, it can only be hoped, that time will bring a more enlightened and kinder feeling. Meanwhile it rests upon those, who care for the preservation of religious faith, to do their part as citizens

to remove prejudice. This prejudice rests
on the hollowest of cries, yet one that
always gains the people's ear and excites
their, alarm. Whenever the demand is
heard for sanction and aid to schools with
religious training in their programme, the
cry is raised, " Our great national school
system is in danger!" It rings through
the land and at once rallies multitudes of
people in opposition, who never thought
about the question, who do not even understand what the danger may be, or how, or
whence it is to come.

It will be a duty to say, and to show, to
such people that the national school system
is not in danger, that this cry is as false as
it is captious, that the real danger is loss of
a people's religious faith, and the forfeit to
the nation's detriment, of the greatest
moral force for order and right conduct
in this world.

" The home and the church," it is said
again, " are the places for religious training,
they are sufficient to avert this danger."

No doubt the home and the church bear
their share of good influence upon the
child, but experience shows that this influence does not reach far enough, and as
often as not is more than outweighed by
the loose example which the child witnesses
in the religionless school. The child ought

to be habituated to a reverence for religion, and impressed with its great importance in this life and for the next. But how
expect the child to deem that important,
about which he never hears his teachers
say one word on any of the six days of his
weekly school-life? And if anything is
ever said about it, it is, more often than not,
a sneer from an agnostic teacher, or a
mockery of it in the mouths of his com-
panions. No, it must be taken as generally
true, that unless religious ideas are inter-
woven with the chief occupation of the
child's daily life, he will value them very
little in his riper years. If religion is true,
it is a crime, to contribute to such a result.

It is not, then, unfair to assert, that one
of the greatest dangers to religious belief
in our times is the system of purely worldly
education, imposed on so many countries
to-day, in spite of the unceasing protest of
the oldest church in the world and the two
hundred and fifty millions of its members.

4. Another, and no slight danger, is the
extreme worldliness and luxurious living of
the rich. Think of the vast sums expended
on their purely selfish tastes and pursuits.
Take a peep into those splendid and costly
club-houses — the soft lounge of the Syba-
rite and Epicurean. Think of the floating-
palace pleasure yachts, the gorgeous villas

at the summer resorts, the brilliant equip-
ages and the dazzling toilettes, male and
female. We shudder at the polygamous
Turk, and the unbridled animalism of the
Oriental, but who keeps up those hundreds
of costly and nameless establishments of
licentiousness in every Christian city?
Place side by side in your thoughts, what
you have learned of Christianity and its
counsels, and say what could possibly be
in common between the one picture and
the other? The luxury-loving rich are of
the " eat, drink, to-morrow we die " class,
and their example, like a contagion, spreads
down through the ranks of the less favored
of fortune in a reduced degree. Until these
people wake up to the dread reality, that
here is not the place of final satisfaction
and final reward, that it is a species of most
reckless gambling to stake all on their few
years of present life, faith can find no place
among them or give anything to hope for.

5. Fiction, which is turned out by the ton
to amuse the leisure hour, is another danger.
What does the best of it parade across its
stage as representative of human society?
Why, a thronging crowd of unadulterated
heathens. Even in the exquisitely refined
and delicate stories of Miss Jane Austen,
whom Lord Macaulay so highly praised, and
in the admittedly clean novels of such masters

as Thackeray and Dickens,* you would never for a moment be reminded, that you were reading about the inhabitants of a world, once visited by a Divine Teacher, and a Divine Redeemer.  Say what people may, all this cannot help having the effect of slowly lulling the constant reader into an unholy and unsafe forgetfulness, and forming the fascinated reader into the mould and stamp of his favorite hero and heroine — " These people seem to have got on famously without much ado about religion, why not I? " — he is apt to say.

The returning agnostic must not fail to take account of these five dangers, and healthily exercise his faith in not only avoiding, but doing battle against their deadly tendencies.

In the following brief chapter, I offer a few hints to smooth the way for some minds, whom the many mysteries of faith hinder and perplex — without reason as will be seen.

---

* Just "to save his face," as the Chinese say, Dickens has a few, very few, allusions to "The Master who was gentle and forgiving," etc.

# CHAPTER XII.

## Mysteries.

We have to swallow a lot of " camels "
in this world around us, why hesitate about
a few more?

From where I am now sitting I can see,
in a bee line, the great Lick observatory —
sixteen atmospheric miles away; it is thirty-
two by the road. It looks just like a coach
and six on the summit of the range. Yet
I know that under that little white dome,
there is the largest telescope yet mounted
in the world; and there are sidereal teles-
copes, elaborate photographic instruments,
quadrants, sextants, true meridians — what
not? There is a trained staff of observers
and distinguished mathematicians, who live
up there in six months of cloud and snow,
five thousand feet above the heads, and
away from the converse of their fellows, to
discover for us the secrets of the stars. It
cost nearly a million dollars to install that
small establishment. And how little, how
very little, they have been able to tell
us; and without at all depreciating their
great devotedness and industry — how useless in the practical affairs of men has even
*that little* proved to be! They have given

us a few pictures. .But as well photograph
a " Fruit-vale " orange or a squash-melon,
for all those pictures tell, in reality, of
Mars or the moon. It was up there they
discovered the fifth moon of Jupiter, a fact
which Professor Ball informed his readers,
in the *London News*, was of "vast importance." In the hard realities of life
and its personal concerns, what is it to me
whether Jupiter has five moons or fifty?
They make stupendous calculations about
the distances, the gravity and motions of
planets, stars, double stars, comets and
nebulae. Curious no doubt, but they are
still gazing into mystery, and are as far
from solving the familiar riddles close
around them as ever. They have made
great advances in knowledge of the sun.
But who will tell us what heat really is, and
why it acts so peculiarly? That sun is one
million times the bulk of our earth; it is
ninety-three millions of miles distant — very
well. The flood of heat, cast out by a bulk
like that, ought to entirely envelope and
keep in equal warmth all parts of a small
globe like the earth. So one would fancy.
But ask Dr. Nansen to tell you what he
saw and felt last year at the North Pole.
No obliquity of the earth's axis can entirely satisfy one, as an explanation of that.
But here is the real mystery of heat. It

travels all the ninety-three millions of miles to come to us — and for all that distance up to within a few feet *it is cold, icy cold* — proof; rise up straight into that sunshine in a balloon; in an hour or two you will be a frost-bitten corpse, the same sun still shining on you! Yet, what enormous initial heat must have been projected to warm that little bed out there in the garden, and make those spring flowers look so gay this morning! Last week Professor Holden and his friends up at the "Lick" had several feet of snow all round them, while we were sitting in shirt sleeves and wearing sunhats from the heat down here! The illustration of the glass of a hot-house usually offered in explanation of this, solves not, for me, the mystery why a thing that was icy cold becomes blazing hot by mere contact with the atmosphere, or by coming under it, so to speak. Yet you *believe* in heat. It is a thing that will blister you, if you do not believe in it. You, at the same time, really know nothing at all about the *thing itself*.

Up at that "Lick," they will tell you the weight of this great earth — enormous — the figures in pounds would reach from here to there. Yet this tremendous bulk is floating about in, apparently, nothing! When we lie down upon it at

night, or step abroad upon it in the day,
how do we know it will not give way under
us and leave us there? We do not know
at all, because everybody will tell you, if
they are straight and honest, that *au fond*
it is a mystery to us, yet you *believe* it will
not give way, you never heard of such a
thing. Centripetal and centrifugal forces —
attraction and gravitation — keep it up.
Yes, of course, but what really is the *thing*,
the *res* of that force, no one ever has told,
or ever will be able to tell us.

Again, this earth is round. Some belated people will say it is not, but I know
it is, because some years ago I left the
shore of that neighboring bay of San Francisco on the train, traveling eastward, and
without ever turning back, I sailed in again
through its Golden Gate, at an exactly op-
posite point of the compass! Well, two-
thirds of its vast, round surface is water;
why doesn't it spill? In the twenty-four
days' stretch across the great Pacific, we
all *believed* it would not spill, but *why*, not
a soul of us knew. Of course, most of us
did know about "diurnal motion," and
"pressure of atmosphere," and such other
school-boy explanation, but the whole vast
phenomenon, its currents and the nicety of
its tidal arrangements, who can ever com-
prehend?

While I write, too, there is a beautiful little creeper called the " Bridal-veil " silently throwing its small, tender tentacles around that porch there, climbing the training laths as skillfully as a sailor-boy shins a halyard. What is it makes it do that? What is the force within it which pushes and guides? We all *believed* it would surely do that, as soon as this spring-time was old enough, and the birds were singing again — but *how*, the wisest of us do not *know*.

These and a score of other things " as familiar as household words " mystify us, yet we delight to believe in them, all because they give us delight. And yet we grumble, and question, and doubt, and say we can not possibly believe a few other mysterious or miraculous things, because we cannot see through them at once. How absurd of us! And they come to us, too, on a word we ought to respect — at least that millions, as good as we, did respect and believe. It is backed, moreover, by a promise that if we but be humbly patient enough, this film-covered glass, through which the light comes only very " darkly," will some day be shattered, and the whole infinite range of knowledge and its unraveled secrets will be in full view, with a whole eternity to revel in — satiating this craving of ours to know. It is worth waiting for, ever so patiently — ever so humbly, is it not? and vastly better, you will agree, than the "exterior darkness" where the other people are to be forever, who are both impatient and proud.

---

The men of science object, that in matters of faith or belief, we surrender our reason. There is a fallacy, and not an honest one, in that assertion. It is not our reason we surrender. It is our understanding. Our reason supplies us with valid and sufficient motives for believing what we cannot understand even in the common things of life. Our reason we are never forbidden to use, but many objects are withdrawn from our understanding, and though it cannot always serve us, it is no hindrance to our belief.

---

## CHAPTER XIII.

### Further Difficulties and Their Answers.

There are particular points of doctrine which some allege to be a block in the way of their unbelieving, or at least a cause of their doubting and their unrest of mind.

With such persons I have had no small experience.  I have met them on the highways of the world — on the decks of ocean steamers, in railways and stage-coaches, in out-of-the-way towns of the New World, on lonely sheep-farms, in hotels and in private homes.

It may be useful to relate this experience, and it may prove helpful to others like them, to subjoin the answers to their difficulties.

I remember a young person on board the S. S. *Rhotomahana* coasting around New Zealand, saying so earnestly:  "If I could only know for certain what God wants me to do, there is nothing, it seems to me, that I would not do for Him.  *  *  * No, no, not what is in books or what men say — I want Him to tell me Himself."

*Reply*. — You want what nobody else in the world is privileged to have — private revelation, is that reasonable?  He certainly gave instructions, fully enough, what each one is to do — they have been handed down by tradition accurately enough.   True, men have confused some parts of them — but still on proper inquiry they are determinable and millions agree about them — unreasonable expectation is foolish and futile.

I remember the wealthy young *squatter*,

as the *Arumac* drew out from wharf to re-
sume her Australian coasting trip, looking
wearily over the busy scene and saying,
"What is the meaning of it all ? "—that
is, the life of men — the world we had been
discussing.

*Reply.* — Unaided by information from the
Author of it we never can know. Hence
the need of revelation, and our duty to
consult it and submit to what it tells
us. Guesses from the data around us
will never answer your question.

I remember the celebrated meteorologist
laying down for a smoking-room audience—
a sympathetic one — in mid-ocean, that
the only comfortable way to live was just
to follow all the instincts of nature when it
can be conveniently done, they must be
right,'else we should not have them.

*Reply.* — It is honorable to be a naturalist
in botany and the laws of storms as you
are — but dishonor and shame and re-
morse are sure to follow the naturalism
you advocate outside your profession —
there is nothing more certain than that,
as abundant experience around us in the
world shows, law courts and jails are the
sad necessities imposed by the " instincts
of nature " that you would have men
follow when it pleased them — therefore
there is something wrong with nature —

human nature — in many respects, since
it leads to such disaster. It needs restraint and discipline, and only when
corrected by a higher teaching, it can be
trusted at all.

I remember the young American sugar-
planter, exiled in the tropics, guessing that
whoever put him in this world would " look
after him all right," and if he were to go
on existing forever, the same disposer of
him would no doubt continue to do so, he
" guessed he'd leave it just like that."

*Reply.* — If He put you here just like a
piece of furniture — a table or a rocking-
chair, no doubt he would; but if he put
you here, and gave you the means ex-
pressly designed for looking after yourself, do not be too sure that He will not
hold you responsible for not making use
of them. And that you could not possibly make a mistake about it, He told you
that way he wanted you and expected
you to use them, in looking after yourself — at least thousands of your fellow-
beings — intelligent fellow-beings—quite
as intelligent as you, perhaps much more
so, think He has. An English writer of
repute declared, that he " would rather
be an atheist and believe there was no
God, than believe there was a God who
having created rational beings, gave

them no intimation of His will, nor made
any communication to them whatever —
the former is a daring creed, but the
other is a foolish one."

I remember the famous humorist — serious
for the moment, while we plowed the
Atlantic, wanting to know how the God,
represented to us by the preachers, could
be a possibility in view of such a world as
this is : and the English mechanic-engineer
saying with an air of relief, but as if the
relief were not quite comfortable, " Yes, a
good many people now say there is no such
being at all."

*Reply.* — The humorist in question is a
well-known *persifleur* of religion — perhaps since Voltaire's time no other author — certainly none in the English
tongue, has done so much harm to religious belief, by sneers veneered with
wit, than he. He acknowledged on that
very afternoon that he had passed a most
irreligious youth — got no instruction
and knew nothing of religion, but what
he afterwards picked up himself. Besides, on his own admission, and to judge
from a few choice personal anecdotes,
that portion of his existence had been
none of the cleanest. However, I told
him he was going against the universal
sense of mankind in every time and place,

which is not a safe thing to do, and that the reason this world, as it is, did not better reflect the Supreme Being in all His goodness, was owing to the gift of free will to men, and the exceedingly bad use that was made of it — " bringing death into the world and all our woe — " and the bad use that many still continue to make of it. For our friend the engine-maker, I might have quoted the opening of a certain Psalm — " The fool says in his heart there is no God." But if any good is to be done to such people you must never be offensive to them. Prove to them there *is* a God by the very necessity of the case — no other way of accounting for our world and its teeming life.

I remember the exceedingly agreeable and perfectly gentlemanly young " station owner," fond of reading in the lonely evenings to the sound of the Pacific surf; very advanced in his opinions about " pre-historic man " and the myths of revelation. Though reared in the Church of England and married to a convent-educated and Catholic wife, he declared his utter inability to believe what his Christian neighbors seemed to do so easily.

*Reply.* — See the danger of reading books by subtle and accomplished speculators without any previous training for argument, and never having heard the proper explanations of the leading facts of revelation. Pre-historic man solves no mystery of the creation — it pushes it back a step, that's all.

But pre-historic man has by no means been certainly discovered. He has turned out to be a mistake of the geologists, or at least many skilled in that *experimental investigation* — geology — it can hardly be called a science, certainly not an exact one — admit, that the evidence for him is only slenderly partial — therefore entirely inconclusive. Thirdly, what does it matter to us, as a practical question, how old our race is; the individual responsibility for individual conduct remains for each one of us, and that is what should chiefly occupy our attention. Again, we should be chary of talking of myths, where so much that is mysterious and inexplicable to us, lies under our very eyes all around. There is a point in all human reasoning, where something must be taken without proof, if reason itself is not to sink into the void where folly reigns, and madness rages.

As to inability to believe like his neighbors — were he as humble as they

were; had he confessed his sins and re-
pented of them as they had; had he
quietly and trustfully prayed daily as
they do, belief would have been as easy
to him as to them. *Without those
things it is easy to no one.* Nor is the
question of personal sin a rash judgment. Without certain fixed moral re-
straints and instructive guidance in
youth, it is impossible for any one to
escape falling into temptation, and having sinned, and sin remaining, a parti-
tion is raised between God and the soul.
Until that is removed the peace of believing will never come. It was not for
nothing we were told, "Blessed are the
clean of heart for they shall see God."
This implies its converse, Unblessed are
the unclean of heart, for they cannot see
God.

I remember the Queensland "slop-shop"
keeper who told me to write him down an
atheist. He said this was a country of free
thought, and he did not want any more
trouble than his business gave him.

*Reply.* — True, every one was free, *before
the law*, to think as he pleased, but there
was a higher law before which he was
not free, else why did he not with equal
freedom *think he was not to die;* think
that he could arrange for his continued

existence just as it suited him ; that, he could not do. Therefore, there *was* a Power superior to him of which he had better take account. His business no doubt demanded attention and should have it, but a day would come when business and all he ever gained by it, should stay behind, and he would have to go forth alone, as little consulted as when he was sent here. Is it not a little daring, then, to brave a Power so much greater than he, and not try to find out what that Power requires to be done, beyond mere business, which is not the ultimate end of man?

I remember the old fellow on an American "ranch" who boasted — being then in the very "sere leaf," indeed — that he *never had done anything wrong* (in his numerous family such a thing as prayer was unknown) ; he was not afraid to die. He had been pretty successful after a hard struggle in this life, and if there happened to be another life, he would struggle there too, and no doubt meet with the same success. Moreover, he had been a good Mason and everybody knew that the Free Masons were too great a body to fear anything or anybody? " *They* were all right."

*Reply.* — A seared conscience is the greatest of calamities. It is the eternal judg-

ment already passed.  It is a most difficult thing to revivify with new sap.  But
it is the only chance.  It may be done
by convincing this self-satisfied soul that
he had done wrong, by omission for instance.  " Remember to keep holy My
Sabbath day," was that never infringed
in course of your long life?  " Thou
shalt adore thy God and Him only shalt
thou serve."  You rarely, if ever, even
acknowledged Him by prayer, and so
forth.  As for that confidence in the
great Masonic body, be not deceived
about their importance or help.  Why,
they were unheard of before the seventeenth century and originated among the
Socinians and other free-thought Protestants of these comparatively recent times.
As a mutual help society you may have
derived certain money benefits from it,
but its methods are suspect to all candid
minds.  If *all* its objects are good why
act like *conspirators* and bind people by
oath and (sometimes) under penalty of
death to secrecy?  It becomes apparent
every day that their methods are either
foolish or wicked.  They are losing caste
among all sensible and respectable people,
and it may be safely predicted that, in
time, this sensational association will die
oblivion's death, like all other absurd

conspiracies. The first notice ever taken
of them by the Popes, was in 1738.
Clement XII. explained who they were,
and what were their objects, and forbade
all Catholics to have anything to do with
them. If they had existed *always*
throughout Europe is it likely that the
watchful head of European society, the
Pope, would never have heard of them
before or noticed them? — most unlikely.

This condition of soul in old age always
arises, from keeping the mind in culpable
religious ignorance through life. If
people would read even the Catechism
occasionally this could never happen.

I remember the Colonial young lady —
High school graduate — who professed to
believe in nothing, and was heard to long
for some one to arise who should free the
world from this " bother " about religion. .
*Reply.* — (I regret to say that this case is
but a type of numerous young ladies to
be met in the Colonies, as an outcome of
free, compulsory and secular education.
While I was in Wellington, N. Z., a
young girl of 19 walked out one fine
summer morning from her parents' well-
to-do-home, furnished with sketching
materials, and sat down in the public
park apparently for a practice in drawing, of which she was rather fond. After

a while, she there deliberately took a pistol from her pocket and blew her brains out!)  The best remedy for our young friend, whom everybody admitted to be as amiable as she was fair, turned out to be association with a good Catholic family in which there were well-brought up young girls like herself, who did not preach to her or at her, but who won her by the happy and unostentatious example of their own lives, and in time of need did her a gentle and generous service.

I remember the amiable and hospitable lady born far south of the Equator, who was "trying Theosophy;" liked it very well, but had not got so far as to reconcile herself to the fact that her four beautiful children had already been cats or mice or snakes, may be, in the pre-existence of the second or third *plano-sphere;* her husband was a *Rosecrucian* and very deep in the occult.

*Reply:* — I gave her a "Life of Madame Blavatsky," by a gentleman of St. Petersburg, whose work has been translated into English and published at the cost of the London "Psychical Research Society." That work must conclusively end forever, in all reasonable and respectable minds, the theosophic craze. On

her evidence Madame Blavatsky is proved
to be but a clever adventuress, who did not
stick at the meanest tricks of a charlatan
to deceive and delude her dupes.  This
book may be had from any London book
agent, and is most useful to have just
now to lay *Mahatmas and spooks*.

I remember the man who was puzzled to
know — if Christ were God and came to
redeem the world, why was it not *visibly*
redeemed?  Did the world, as we see it,
look as if it were redeemed?  The world is
full of sin, and suffering, and death.  Then
he told a story of a poor old negro Metho-
dist of Carolina, who had had "salvation"
preached at him all his life, and who was
very religious in his own bothered way;
one day an earthquake happened that shook
things up "pretty considerable" and scared
the old man so that he took to his prayers.
"Oh A'mighty God," he said, "you come
right down heah and fix things up, but
don't you send yo' Son dis time, come
yo'self — dis job is too big and mebbe He
can't do it."  He excused the profanity
by the great simplicity of the poor, old
soul, but he had no doubt but the same
idea was struggling through the old dark-
ey's brain that was such a trouble to his
own mind.  The thing was *de facto* not
accomplished.

*Reply.* — Redemption, as has always been explained, does not, primarily, regard the earthly condition of the race. Its effect is to make it possible for man to regain a title to the " eternal inheritance " — " *facta redemptione* " — the price having been paid for him. The title had been hopelessly lost to him, and infinite reparation was needed — co-equal with the character of Him who was wronged, by revolt against His command. This was done through the Incarnation; and through that alone could it have been effected. But it has not ended man's state of probation — it now gives him a powerful and salutary motive for effort; he is assured that he can earn the great reward, and his earning power, so to speak, is made effective and secure.

It is not accurate to say, that there are no effects visible in the world from the Incarnation and its work. A vast change for the better has come over the lives of men, who by the good use of their free will have lent themselves to the influence of Christianity. Comparisons of Christian lives with the most cultured among ancient peoples, prove this beneficial change beyond all doubt. And the contemporary knowledge we have of peoples not yet Christianized,

affords evidence of Christianity's elevating and civilizing influence. If sin
abounds and its necessary shadow, suffering, it comes from the perverse use of a
will left free to choose evil courses,
which unfortunately the majority do, in
spite of and in opposition to the teachings and protests of Christianity; and so
have apparently discredited by their
conduct the work of the Redemption.
Death for the good is not an evil; you
ought to be a little more advanced in
reasoning power and intelligence than
the "negro from Carolina."

I remember the proprietor of a New Zealand homestead picturesquely situated by
the "wide Pacific strand" — a man of more
than average education, who was very
aggressive against all things of faith. His
mind had even taken an angry turn. His
mother, to whom he had been much at-
tached, had died in the slow suffering of
cancer. This incensed him against the
supernal Power — he used to say, "If I
could only get at it —— !" He assumed
the role of an infidel propagandist on all
occasions, even with his poor workmen.
He had only two children. One had been
baptized by the care of the grandmother,
who was "an Anglican;" when she died
he kept the second unbaptized — as an

experiment to show off against "the other fellow." He had made his gentle and amiable little wife as great an unbeliever as himself.

*Reply.* — He was reared in the Anglican communion. Time has sadly demonstrated that *private judgment* is the portico of the free thought, which means thought utterly unbridled and unlicensed — a thing that is fast making human society unbearable, for reasonable and civilized men. Mrs. Besant, the wife of an Anglican parson, has also informed the world that the sight of her first baby, agonizing in diphtheria, steeled her heart against God and religion. It is as unfair, as it is shallow, to charge to God every particular of the condition of secondary causes who are free agents and *endowed* with *faculties* for *self-help* and *mutual protection.* It looks a fair bargain that the First Cause should have given over a portion of His creation to such agents furnished with sufficient capital, so to speak, to get along. He added to it besides a great liberality of treatment; never interfering with them for their allotted time, withdrawing his visible presence lest it should inconvenience or hamper them in any way; and for all

that only exacting a reasonable service
and acknowledgment. The accidents of
all kinds occurring in this temporary condition of things, (and sickness and
diseases are among them) regard the
secondary agents. To expect Him to
interfere in every case exceeds the limits
of His part of the bargain as a *Provisor
generalis* — the primary Providence. It
is much to have been assured by Him,
that full and just compensation shall
be made to those who submissively
suffer; "*Merces tua magna nimis.*" It
is charged, that it is inhumane in Him
to look on at suffering, *able to relieve
and cure, and not doing so;* even men
would not be so unfeeling were it in
*their* power. But this is making God,
*human* merely. We hear a good deal
from infidels about *anthropomorphism,*
which obtains, say they, when believers
reduce God merely to human dimensions
in their conception of Him. But what
are *they* doing in the case discussed?
Why, they are supposing God to be
exactly like the human being, and blam-
ing Him for not being so. A perpetual
interference for relief of every pang or
pain, no matter how prolonged, would
upset the whole established order, which
no rational being, at present, looks for.

If this state were *final* perhaps we might, with a show of reason, look to Him for help at every turn.   But it is not final, we know; and the general expectation is, that the day of full compensation and explanation will surely come.

With regard to the stupid and *unfair* experiment of this man with his unbaptized boy, the same explanation holds good as was given above about redemption.   The effects await on the action of free will and its use, and the sacrament *chiefly refers to the spiritual order and the eternal future state.*   Baptism is not a visible and miraculous transformation in the present; no one pretends that it is.   The titled poet who returned a Buddhist from Japan, delights to dwell on the superiority of manners and bearing of Japanese children over Christian children.   Besides that this depends on what kind of Christian children he has been acquainted with; he forgets that we learn from other travelers in that country, as intelligently observant as he, that the Japs in general even from a tender age, are the most shamelessly lascivious of peoples — and the Chinese, as is well known, are hardly better.

Finally, with regard to this man's wish "to get at" the great First Cause —

merely to fancy this little five-feet long
creature "getting at" the mighty Maker
of the universe, has something so sub-
limely ludicrous in it, that it would
amuse, if its impiety did not terrify.

I remember the souls troubled about
prayer. One said it was talking into a
great silence; it was hard not to grow
tired of saying things all by yourself, to
which no sound or word was ever heard
in reply; that it required a force of imagi-
nation, which many people do not possess,
to fancy God present with us or listening
when we pray.

*Reply.* — Prayer of course is not like a
human conversation. It is impossible
without faith. Prepared by what faith
teaches about it; that there is a God
who is interested in us because he owns
us; who wishes us to look on Him as
a Father, and expects us to depend on
and confide in Him; who is all powerful, able, and willing to help in all things
for our good — then with such conviction
in mind, it will appear far from talking
into void, or tiresome or needing *imagina-
tion.* At the same time every one must
confess to a kind of natural need of com-
muning about himself with *some one.*
This comes from the fact of our individ-
uality. The peculiar and distinct per-

sonality each one has, makes us uncom-
fortable to feel alone and isolated amid
accidents and fortunes of a temporary
existence. This is a natural pre-disposi-
tion to prayer. It is evidenced in the child
telling all about its little self and its concerns to its mother or its care-taker.
Nor does the same want ever leave the
man, which proves the reasonableness of
the assertions of faith.

Another had given up prayer because it
seems so unmanly — cowardly in fact — to
grovel perpetually, to bepraise and beg.

*Reply.* — An unmanly or cowardly act is
to refuse to face a danger, or to endure
a hardship, or to shirk a painful or laborious task, when duty and a greater good
call on us to do and dare. Where do we
do any of these mean things in prayer?
We feel our dependence, knowing we
have been created by a Power superior
to ourselves, exalting the qualities of
that Creator, idealizing His great and
good attributes, is so far from groveling
that it exalts our idea of ourselves — in-
creases our esteem for ourselves and
gives us courage. It is only fair and
just in us and manly too, to acknowledge
our dependence. We ask to be
strengthened as to what He wants us to
do, and make ready to do it at any cost

true, but prayers of all kinds, no matter
how long, are nothing but the expan-
sion of that divine compendium, as
ascetic writers often demonstrated.

Another adduced puzzling cases of people
who prayed long and earnestly for a manifestly good thing and were not heard —
one especially about people weakly addicted
to the drink habit. He had known some
who were so ashamed and conscious of that
terrible weakness, that they left nothing
undone, followed strictly every spiritual
advice, novenas, communions, confessions,
for help, and to no avail — they fell again
and again.

*Reply.* — It is nowhere taught that miracles follow prayers on all occasions.
Neither must it be looked for, that
prayer should result in loss of will-
power in the petitioner in any given action or habit — one's will is not suddenly
taken away and grace substituted for it.
We must be satisfied to struggle against
temptation aided by grace, with a will
very much inclined to the evil *whose
habit we culpably* began.

In the case cited there were relapses, it
is true, but to my knowledge there were
intervals of abstention and improvement,
and that was a decided gain. We can
not know the workings of an individual

soul, or what flaw there may be in its disposition, to account for failure, but it is there, be assured, lies the cause. Our Lord promised that everything we ask the Father in His name shall be granted — yes, but it must be in every-thing — in matter and disposition — entirely worthy of the holy name we ask in.

I remember the soul distressed by the sight of a crucifix; the thought would keep rising, What kind of a Being or Justice can that be, who could look upon a spectacle so horrible and be pleased or placated or appeased by it or even accept it at all? Then the question would come — If that is God — if Christ is God — have we not the curious situation of God *offering Himself to Himself* — Himself suffering that His own self or His own Justice may be satisfied? There are souls who would rather suffer any loss themselves than accept anything so cruel from another.

*Reply.*—This opens up the whole mystery of the Incarnation, and it is a very great one. We can never hope to fathom that here below. Convince yourself of having been assured on very good authority, accepted by millions as wise as you, that unless that happened it would fare very badly with you and with all this world. Relieve yourself also with the opinion,

that all the cruel details of that sacrifice
were not essential, because a word — an
act — one tear of a *divine* and *human
person*, would have been price enough
for many condemned races — all his
actions being of infinite value — but
Christ chose Himself to undergo them
to increase men's notion of the great
guilt of sin and offer a striking contra-
diction in His own person to pride, lust,
and guilty indulgences, to which all men
are, as everybody knows, and as he
foreknew, so prone.

It is not accurate to say that God offered Himself to Himself barely. There
was present in the offering the human
nature which He assumed suffering, too,
and whose suffering clothed round by a
divine personality, became infinite in value
and co-equal with the magnitude of an of-
fense done to infinite justice and majesty.
About souls suffering loss rather than
accept for themselves so cruel a sacrifice — they little know what they are
talking about. On the assurance of
revelation there is nothing more certain
than that, if that loss did overtake them,
they would be eternally sorry for their
pride-inspired and ignorant folly.

I remember others disturbed by reading
about the world in the time of Christ. It

was in a very bad state — there were teeming populations in the Farther East, in
India, Thibet, China, Japan — Brahmins,
Buddhists, Confucians, Shinto idol wor-
shipers.   Black Africa was crowded with
naked savage cannibals reveling in lust,
slaughter, blood, cruelty — worse than the
horrors there to-day, no doubt.   The vast
Roman Empire had altars for impure idols
and temples for a hundred gods.   The
islands of antipodean seas were peopled as
now,   with   fearful   flesh-eating   tribes.
Christ came to teach and to save all, yet
He seemed to take no care at all about these
hundreds of millions, living and dying while
He lived.   He never alluded to their existence.   His   work   was   restricted — very
local.   A very small number knew he was
there at all, and fewer still knew him for
the Messiah, and when He died, notwithstanding all His miracles, scarcely any at
all believed or were converted.

*Reply.* — The same difficulty shadows the
   whole history of the Jews.   It lies in the
   words *chosen people.*   The fact is certainly before us that they were divinely
   favored before all other and more numerous peoples.   At the same time it clears
   away a good deal of the mystery to
   remember that *all* peoples in the far-back
   centuries were Hebrews once — all of the

one stock. The human race was once
small in number, but in the growth and
vast increase there was a dispersion-pro-
cess and a winnowing according to
deserts; and God dealt to each the measure of His justice and treatment of His
wisdom, just as they deserved from Him.
Abraham and his seed deserved best from
Him and so were made His favored
agents. The rest were permitted to
wander apart and left to their own
devices, just as we see most of them
*still* — yellow, red, brown and black
men — idolaters and cannibals.

Christ did not choose to appear simul-
taneously and preach to them all, though
being divine, He might have done
so, it is true. Equally true that millions still remain ignorant of Him and
His divine mission. But to argue with
justice from this and similar facts,
regarding peoples, we should know the
whole state of the case — concerning
the history of their conduct and deal-
ings with God. Manifestly we do not
know, and never can know that; so it is
but reasonable to assume a neutral, if a
waiting, attitude. Had Christ come in
that clearly superhuman character, then
the present order of trial would have there
and then ended. Belief should have been

compelled, and faith dispensed with.
That kind of coming, however, is promised and will happen — when all things
shall be made manifest.

As to the fewness of the converted,
notwithstanding all the miracles our Lord
performed, it must be remembered that
the immense numbers — 5,000 after one
sermon and 3,000 after another — who
became Christians immediately on the
apostle's preaching Christ crucified and
risen, must have been those who had seen
Him and witnessed His miracles, and
some the subjects of them in their own
persons, else they would never have
yielded so readily.

I remember those again who were sad-
dened in mind and doubtful of a divine
goodness by the cruelties of life; the hid-
eous deformities and diseases, the slow
agony of wasting cancers and leprosy and
the like; the blood-thirstiness that breaks
out in all mankind, savage and civilized
alike; then the cruelties of the animal
world; all the fierce beasts and poisonous
things; tigers, lions, snakes, jaguars, wild
elephants, sharks and sword-fish, vultures,
hawks, eagles — the butcher bird that
impales its living food on a thorn and
sits watching its writhings — the sea louse
that eats into the spinal marrow of the

whale and drives the monster mad — the
Kea of New Zealand that digs its beak into
the flesh of the live sheep for the kidney
fat and only that — who gave them all
those pitiless instincts?

*Reply.* — Why should such things trouble
*your* mind? Have you personally any
great reason to complain of God's goodness to you? If unhappily there are
people subject to the fearful ills that
flesh is heir to, as a consequence of the
aboriginal blight of evil, has not God
imparted instincts of compassion and
mutual help to his creatures? All are
not so afflicted — far from it — only the
few, very few, comparatively, and it
*generally* comes from the accidents oc-
casioned by secondary causes; and is it
not beautiful to see the sane always
ready to succor the unsound, exhibit-
ing rare and unselfish virtue, and confer-
ring comparative happiness on the afflicted? Men are thus made the vice-
regents — the secondary Providence of
God to one another in the world. The
old scholastics have discussed the animals and their ways. It was their opinion that, having been made for man, and
originally subject to him, it was part of
his penalty when he fell, that the animals
should break away from him into a wild

state and become his enemies, and thus
diverted, by his fault, from their original
destination, they have ramped about,
soured — lost — waste parts of the creation, in fact, ever since; but the Creator
has not left man at their mercy; man
still holds the upper hand, in the main,
as everybody knows.

Human blood-thirstiness is the ruinous
part of a structure that once was noble,
and which still shows not unsightly bits
of what it originally was. It can only be
accounted for on the ground *of the fall
into moral evil* — the failure in the first
trial of free will — another part of sin's
penalty.

The instances of set and deliberate
cruelty of animals are far from being
authenticated, nor are such practises uni-
form and habitual. A sheep farmer of
long experience in New Zealand told me,
that the Kea bird learned to locate the
kidney fat of the sheep from his habit of
prowling about the station slaughter-yard
and picking at the sheep-skins spread
out to dry with the wool down. The
most toothsome bit was this fat in the
region of the kidneys or liver, and when
the skins were not there to be picked, he
went for the sheep on the hills and locat-
ing the part where he got his so-appe-

tizing morsel, he fastened his claws in the wool and sunk his beak in the soft flesh above the haunches, even then he did not always strike the fat directly either, or neatly! Other birds, from imitative habit, copied the knowing ones and so this curious custom of theirs came to be.

For the rest, what are animals to you; you have not created them; you are not responsible for them? They are very near us, and they are as far away from us as mystery; they are strangers to us in reality. They live their own peculiar life and there's an end of it.

I remember others, and they were many, who were incensed against the doctrine of Hell. Some felt that a Being who could look on at the tortures of his own creature for eternity, could not be an object of any one's love, admiration and adoration; others, that they were doing God a service, vindicating Him, by repudiating what they called a horrible doctrine; others asserted that it was a fiction invented by men to hold other men in subjection by force of terror — a horrid nightmare imposed on human minds by the designing and so on. *Reply.*— No doubt Hell is an awful doctrine. No use in saying that it is easy to be calmly reconciled to it. But there

is no use either in denying it.  Viewing
the minds of men as a whole, we find
that in every time, it formed an inseparable
portion of religious belief.  This ex-
trinsic evidence throws doubt at once on
your denial.  And the thing is so awful
that — presented even as doubtful — it
should urge every one to take no risk, to
seek further and make himself very sure
that he is making no mistake about what
may result in such a frightful disaster to
himself.  For it is said to be eternal and
a punishment.

Then he should remember that if this
be so, no amount of assertion or repudia-
tion on his part can in the least alter *the
fact*.  And if our Lord ever revealed
anything about the unseen in unmistakable terms, it was this sombre fact.

There is one comfort at any rate.  We
are not there yet, and there are ways of
escaping going there.  And the ways are
so well known and within such easy
reach, that we can be morally sure of
never having to go there, if we like.

The only reason why any one goes to
that dreadful place, is that he departs
from life in a state of overt rebellion
and contempt for the great Creator, who
gave him his being.  Where else could
he go?  Surely he could not expect to

be cordially greeted and richly rewarded and welcomed hospitably, after such reckless and daring conduct as his.  Those who have power in this world are not accustomed to welcome to their homes, and dine, and be hail-fellows with the men who despise their authority and trample on the laws — such a thing was never heard of.  Do you think it will be any different in the realm beyond the grave? The love of God comes irresistibly with serving him and acknowledging Him — above all, with a good conscience.  The truth is, a good deal of this questioning about Hell arises from *not* having a good conscience and knowing very well why — having got into scrapes by sinning freely, it takes a lot of whistling to keep up courage, like the boy passing through the graveyard.  When you pass in your walks by a convict-prison, you know very well there is a painful state of things going on there — fellow-beings undergoing severe and often dreadful punishment. You return to your dinner none the less with appetite unimpaired.  You do not rail against the judge and are not the least angry with the jury who convicted. Why?  Because you very sensibly say — Justice demanded it.  " But it need not be eternal," you say.  To assert that, you must

be in a position to understand all about
God's justice, which you are not, *that* being infinite, and above our limited comprehension. Besides, between you and
me, is there anything less than the sanction of *eternal* punishment that will restrain the run of men from vice? You
know there is not. Your rearrangement
of things for God, is, to say it without
wishing to be impolite, an impertinence.
It does not concern us ; we are not masters here. If there is one thing clearer
than another, it is that we are wholly de-
pendent — otherwise we could settle down
comfortably and arrange to stay in life as
long as we pleased. But we cannot stay.
Some one will call some day. So it is
wisest to prepare to go in submission,
and you may be sure everything will be
right with us.

The general disposition of things here
below and our destinies are not in our
hands, but it is given to us to make the
best of them and, turning them to our
advantage, we need not go to Hell.

But enough — the famous and devout
author of the " Imitation " propounds
rather dogmatically that " they who travel
much are *rarely* (without the emphasis)
sanctified " — by the way, how did he
know since he never went anywhere? —

but be that as it may, the widely-traveled meet, by the waysides and on the high-roads of life, many odd specimens of humanity and fall in with curious phases of human psychology. If their experiences take a little of the spiritual shine off themselves, there is left them a compensation from the good, or instruction, or pleasure that others may derive from reading those experiences even in the very humble way here presented.

THE END.